WITCH
LEGEND OF THE SILVER HUNTER
BOOK TWO

Cover Design: Keith Martin, Imperial Graphics
Edited by: Shannon A. Thompson

ISBN-10: 099652651X
ISBN-13: 978-0-9965265-1-7

PUBLISHER'S NOTE

License Notes

CONTENTS

ACKNOWLEDGMENTS

I want to give a big thank you once again to my partner for giving me the time to focus on being creative over the last year. Thanks, Tiger.

Big shout out to my Beta Reader, Lisa Cullinan.

PROLOGUE

Kieran strode into the council chamber with such force the doors slammed into the walls. The Matriarchs rose at the interruption of their meeting. All except Kieran's grandmother who remained seated in her throne-like chair. When he reached the end of the conference table, Kieran smacked his hand down on top of it, and the room echoed with the sound.

"We did not summon you, boy. A tracker does not bring business before this council."

"Shut up, Aunt Fiona. I'm not here as a tracker of the House of Beauty. I'm here as the hunter-candidate. Time is up, Grandmother. You are all out of granddaughters to send to their deaths. The pact is broken, and the mongrels of the forest murdered my sisters."

"Sit down, now! My grandson makes a valid point. We lived to witness a cursed generation when we must allow a male to test as a hunter. We must also resign ourselves to this fate. Kieran is the last of the House of Beauty. With his death, our line ends."

"I'm not dying any time soon, old woman. I've got too much to live for. Oh, I'm so much more than my sisters."

"A disappointment is what you are, boy."

"Only to a closed-minded old woman, who couldn't do what was needed to be done before she let an entire generation of huntresses be slaughtered. Serena and Rosie both died as full huntresses. My other sisters were never given the chance to properly test. The Alpha who rules this pack now is a direct descendant of the Beast himself. I'm the only one who stands a chance to defeat him."

"Male arrogance. Your chances of defeating a monster of such an ancient a lineage are less than even your sisters."

BEAUTY'S TALE

All at once, the merchant lost his whole fortune, excepting a small country house at a great distance from town, and told his children with tears in his eyes, they must go to there and work for their living...Poor Beauty at first was sadly grieved at the loss of her fortune; "but," said to herself, "were I to cry ever so much, that would not make things better, I must try to make myself happy without a fortune." When they came to their country house, the merchant and his three sons applied themselves to husbandry and tillage; and Beauty rose at four in the morning, and made haste to have the house clean, and dinner ready for the family. In the beginning she found it very difficult, for she had not been used to work as a servant, but in less than two months, she grew stronger and healthier than ever. After she had done her work, she read, played on the harpsichord, or else sung whilst she spun. On the contrary, her two sisters did not know how to spend their time; they got up at ten, and did nothing but saunter about the whole day, lamenting the loss of their fine clothes and acquaintance. "Do but see our youngest sister," said they, one to the other, "what a poor, stupid, mean-spirited creature she is, to be contented with such an unhappy dismal situation."

"Beauty and the Beast" by Jeanne-Marie Le Prince de Beaumont, 1757 English translation."

Those of you who follow me as chronicler of the House of Beauty must continue the tradition of keeping the truth in these records secret from all but the huntress of the house. In some cases, keeping secrets will be best if even the huntress remains unaware of some events. Mother became a bitter woman when she founded our house. I am aware how the stories portray her as bright and cheerful. After all, I helped craft some of those stories. She resented her life and her sisters most of all. She never expected to marry into royalty. At best, she figured on marrying a farmer. Shortly after, mother convinced father marriage to her would be in his best interests and lost touch with her youngest brother. No trace of my youngest uncle can be found, although rumors are often carried to us of his marriage to the daughter of a count in a distant land.

The first entry from the first chronicles of the House of Beauty, translated in the nineteenth century from the original French.

CHAPTER ONE:

The brown minivan pulled into a gas station in Bangor, Maine after a week and a half on the road from Little Rock, Arkansas. The trip shouldn't take so long, but the young lovers driving the van stopped often to explore the sights and to work a couple of tracking jobs. After rolling the van to a stop at the pumps, the driver put the van in park and shut off the engine. After opening his door, Kieran, a tall man in his early twenties, dressed in blue jeans, a black t-shirt, and sneakers, emerged; his long black hair flowed down his back to below his firm ass. Out of the passenger side stepped Cory, a man in his mid-twenties, his blond hair and beard trimmed short, also dressed in jeans, a t-shirt, and sneakers. The blond opened the rear passenger door and a huge black wolf leapt from the car, a silver collar with a wolf's head clasp hung around its neck. The boyfriends glanced at each other across the roof of the station wagon, and with a knowing nod, Kieran turned to the pump, putting gas in the car. Cory signaled the wolf and crossed the parking lot to an open grassy area where the wolf relieved himself. Once the wolf finished, they returned to the car, and the blond put him back in the car before heading to the gas station's store for supplies and the restroom.

Cory returned and put the supplies into the car as Kieran finished pumping gas. His dark-haired companion crossed the lot to the store for his own turn in the restroom; when he returned, they continued on their way.

As they left the gas station, Kieran glanced at his boyfriend and could tell what he was thinking.

"We still need to drive for about another hour, Wolf," Kieran said, calling his boyfriend by the nickname he'd given him over Christmas break. "Granddad's family built the place on a secluded section of the coast so no one would bother them."

Cory reached into the backseat and stroked the wolf's head between the ears. Only a few months back the black wolf had been his barely thirteen-year-old nephew Billy Cooper. After Billy's very first shift, the boy had opted to stay in wolf form in order to remain with his Uncle Cory and with Kieran. The silver collar with its wolf head design contained a powerful binding spell, which kept Billy in animal form.

"I hope we'll get time to relax and check out the ocean while we're here. Billy and I would love to visit the ocean."

Cory's voice held a bit of a nervous tremor, causing Kieran doubt over the idea of introducing his boyfriend to his father's family. Perhaps introducing his shifter-related boyfriend to his magic-wielding grandparents and uncle didn't rank as a brilliant idea.

"I'm sure we'll find time to play in the ocean. Granddad's estate owns about two miles of private beach. We can camp out on the beach one night and make love under the stars."

Unless, of course, Kieran thought, *Dad's chasing me around the estate, and I'm dodging the spells he's hurling in my general direction. I can imagine all the fun of trying to make out with my boyfriend while ducking fireballs and other dangerous spells.*

"Camping on the beach sounds like fun. Did you ever go before?"

"Not since I was a kid. Dad and Uncle Brom took about a dozen guys from school and me out camping on the beach one weekend. The trip didn't go well. Turned out a couple of the guys were allergic to shellfish."

Kieran's thoughts refocused on his paternal heritage from his father and grandfather; he was a descendant of the Silver Witch, a figure so wrapped in secrecy not even fairy tales made any mention of the most powerful line of mages the world had ever known. Part of the reason for traveling to Maine was the coming magical challenges. *I wonder when Dad will start the test. With my luck, Dad started the test when we called to tell him we left Arkansas. I hope I can keep Cory and Billy safe until I can go on the offensive.*

CHAPTER TWO

The minivan stopped before an impressive iron gate, the only passage through the looming stone wall, which divided the estate from the rest of the world. Cory winced and Billy the black wolf howled in pain as they crossed through the barrier of Silver magic. Kieran reached out and caught his lover's hand.

"I'm sorry, Cory, the pain will only last a moment longer."

The dark-haired young man quickly keyed in a sequence on the security system. The gates parted, and when they opened wide enough for the van to fit, he drove through. Cory rubbed as his head throbbed with a headache, and Billy the wolf continued to howl his pain as they passed through the barrier. Kieran pulled the van over and pulled his lover to him to help ease the pain. He also reached back to caress the wolf between his ears.

"I'm sorry. I didn't think to shield the van before we got here."

"I think we'll survive. But this is our first time being exposed to so much Silver magic."

"The barrier is designed to keep out shifters and warn of enemy mages. Every generation adds to the power. I didn't get to add to the magic of the barrier yet, which is why you both experienced so much pain."

"Well, we're through, and I'm sure your family will be ready with the pitchforks and flaming torches when we get to the house."

Kieran laughed and put the van back in gear, heading for his grandparents' house. After nearly twenty minutes of driving, Cory wondered if the family put the house on the ground or if Kieran's family lived in trees. Kieran brought the van around yet another bend, and a huge clearing opened up before them. A huge log and glass structure worthy of any high-end resort sprawled across the clearing and back into the woods.

"This is your grandparents' house?" The question escaped Cory's mouth before he stopped himself.

Kieran laughed at his lover's expression. "What? You expected a castle where Sleeping Beauty would be right at home?"

"To tell you the truth, I couldn't imagine what to expect. Don't ask why but the only picture in my mind is of your grandparents living in a dark forbidding castle with a moat and a dragon guarding the gates. So I guess you're more the woodsman than Prince Charming."

Cory couldn't help laugh at Kieran's expression as the Prince Charming line sank home.

"Your sense of humor is tragic, Wolf. As a shifter, you should be careful about any references to stories with a big bad wolf in them. Remember, what's a fairy tale for you is family history for me."

Cory cut off in mid-laugh as Kieran's comment registered. Try as he might, Cory still didn't think of *Beauty and the Beast* as based in historical fact. How do you deal with a fairy tale made flesh and blood?

Kieran pulled the van up to the front of the giant cabin. Kieran's father and another slightly older and bearded man of similar appearance met the young men. Kieran seemed to teleport from his side of the van to wrap the second man in a fierce hug. The man hugged back as Kieran's father shook hands with Cory and patted the wolf on the head.

"Welcome to my family's home, Cory."

"Thank you, Kellen. The place is impressive."

Kellen's laugh rang silver off the walls of the cabin. Kieran and the older man he hugged glanced over at Kellen and Cory, and Kieran's laugh joined his father's as he recognized the expression on Cory's face. Releasing the older man, Kieran crossed to his lover and drew him into a fierce kiss.

"Forgive, Cory, Dad. He thought Gramps and Grams lived in a dark and forbidding castle. He's got his fairy tales mixed up."

"Well, with a little warning beforehand, we could have whipped up a good glamour of ancient and dusty ruins for him. A moldy old castle appears kind of silly in the middle of the Maine woods, but anything to excite the tourists," said the older man Kieran hugged on arrival.

"So, introductions. Cory, you already met my father, Kellen. This rogue here is his older brother and my favorite uncle, Brom. Uncle Brom, this is my boyfriend, Corwin Cooper. Cory for short."

"A pleasure to finally meet you, sir."

"You can call me Brom, or even Uncle Brom, Cory."

The two shook hands, and Brom stopped and raised Cory's hand so he might study the ring on the young man's finger. He grabbed Kieran's hand and brought the matching rings up to examine closely.

The rings on the boys' fingers flashed as the sunlight caught the amber and diamond eyes of the nearly twin double wolf heads on both rings. He was surprised to see what the spells he'd forged into the plain silver bands had transformed them into. Kieran had designed special spells for what he called his true love rings. While he'd crafted the rings and cast the spells into them, Brom didn't even begin to think he understood the magic his nephew had designed. Brom glanced at his younger brother before turning his focus back at the young men before him. Before he spoke, the huge black wolf, which arrived with the young lovers, nudged his head, searching for attention.

Uncle Brom started looking over the young man his nephew had brought home with a more discerning eye before voicing his concerns. "Okay. I'm confused. Since when does a tracker of the shifter hunting House of Beauty take a shifter for a boyfriend and another as a pet? Talk about being in the wrong fairy tale."

Kieran laughed at his uncle's confusion. He drew Cory into a hug before speaking again. "We moved out of fairy tales and into Shakespeare, Uncle Brom. Some days, our relationship is more of a *Romeo and Juliet* than *Beauty and the Beast*."

"Nephew, your romance sounds more like *Romeo and Juliet* meets *Beauty and the Beast*. I hope this isn't going to end like either of those tales."

"No, sir. Kieran and I are going to get the happily ever after," Cory answered for the young men.

"Well," Brom said to Kieran's father. "Why don't you get your son and his boyfriend settled in? I need to get back to my work at the forge." Brom turned his attention back to his nephew. "I want your input when you get a chance, Kieran."

"Of course, Uncle Brom. You know I can't resist."

Brom hugged his nephew and shook hands with Cory before striding off toward the woods. Kieran turned from watching his uncle walk off and faced his father.

"I guess Cory and I are in the guest cabin."

"Yes, your grandmother thought you boys would like the privacy. Your grandfather would toss you into your old room here in the main house, despite the fact you last used the room when you were fifteen."

"Yeah, the intensity of my training to become a tracker put an end to visits here. I bet nothing in my room changed since the last time I was here, Dad."

"Your grandparents left both our rooms alone, Son. Why don't you two—" A head butt from the wolf reminded Kellen of the third member of the boys' party. "Sorry, why don't you three go get settled into the guest cabin? Dinner will be at seven. Don't be late."

"Yes, sir."

Kieran bundled Cory and Billy the wolf back into the van and set off for the guest cabin hidden behind the main house.

BEAUTY'S TALE

The good merchant was of quite a different opinion; he knew very well that Beauty outshone her sisters, in her person as well as her mind, and admired her humility and industry, but above all her humility and patience; for her sisters not only left her all the work of the house to do, but insulted her every moment. The family had lived about a year in this retirement, when the merchant received a letter with an account of that a vessel, on board which he had effects, was safely arrived. This news had liked to have turned the heads of the two eldest daughters, who immediately flattered themselves with the hopes of returning to town, for they were quite weary of a country life; and when they saw their father ready to set out, they begged of him to buy them new gowns, headdresses, ribbons, and all manner of trifles; but Beauty asked for nothing for she thought to herself, that all the money her father was going to receive, would scarce be sufficient to purchase everything her sisters wanted.

"What would you have, Beauty?" said her father.

"Since you have the goodness to think of me," answered she, "be so kind to bring me a rose, for as none grows hereabouts, they are a kind of rarity." Not that Beauty cared for a rose, but she asked for something, lest she should seem by her example to condemn her sisters' conduct, who would have said she did it only to look particular.

Beauty and the Beast by Jeanne-Marie LePrince de Beaumont, 1757 English translation

The founding Huntress left to her eldest daughter the position of Huntress. Across the ages, the line remained strong until the time of the tenth Huntress. Celestine de la Belle was a woman blessed with many daughters and cursed with a few sons. Her daughters competed to decide who would succeed their mother as Huntress and leader of the House of Beauty. To prevent her children from spilling each other's blood, Celestine created the pact and the test. Celestine found a wolf-shifter clan and bound its Alpha and his line to her service with her gift of Silver magic. The clan would be free to hunt on her lands so long as each generation provided warriors for a test she devised for her heirs. When a daughter of the house reached the age of eighteen, she would be sent out to a special clearing on the first full moon after her birthday to face five shifters in combat. If she killed all five without using her magic, she would become the Huntress of the next generation. Celestine also decided her sons would serve a purpose as well and trained them to track shifters.

She also established the test of the tracker, where each male of the line would track down and kill a shifter of the pack to prove his worth.

An entry from the Fifth Chronicle of the House of Beauty, translated from the original German in the twentieth century.

CHAPTER THREE

Cory stood in awe in front of the guest cabin. The cabin appeared to be about the size of his parents' barn back home. He gazed at his reflection in the wall of glass, which made up the front of the cabin. He also watched his lover as Kieran unloaded their bags from the back of the minivan. Hopping from the back seat of the van, Billy the black wolf padded over to sit beside Cory and pressed his huge head against Cory's leg.

"This place is pretty big, don't you think, Billy?" Cory stroked between the wolf's ears.

Billy huffed his agreement. Kieran placed the bags at the foot of the stairs leading up to the front door of the cabin. Looking at his lover, he only chuckled in amusement at the awe on Cory's beautiful face.

"You realize you gave me the impression of a struggling student trying to make ends meet back in Arkansas, Kieran? Now you show me you come from a family with more wealth than most of the state."

"Oh, I don't think Gramps is richer than everyone in Arkansas; after all, the Walton family lives in Bentonville. None of the money from either family is mine to do anything with—at least, not at the moment. So I needed to earn my own money for school."

"This is still overwhelming, Kieran."

"I realize this is all a bit much, but at least Gramps and the rest of Dad's family don't flaunt their wealth. I think they're embarrassed by how wealthy they are. Each generation goes out and makes their own fortune before they get to enjoy what they will inherit."

"Why bother if they're so rich? Why go out and add more to the pile?"

"Both sides of my family are descended from a merchant family, Cory. The concept of proving you can make your own way in the world is drummed into the genetics of Dad's family for centuries."

"Well, rich or poor, I still love you, Kieran Belle."

"Good, because I love you too, Corwin Cooper," said Kieran in one of his rare usages of Cory's full name. "Come on and help me get our stuff inside. Grams will take our heads if we're late for dinner the first night we're here." Kieran decided not to mention to his lover about his concerns regarding his father and uncle. Something about their demeanor when he'd arrived with Cory seemed off. He wondered if Gramps was pushing the prophecy again.

INTERLUDE: FAMILY PLOTS

Brom arrived at the main house an hour before dinner was scheduled to start at the request of his father and brother. He entered to find the house filled with the aroma of his mother's cooking. From the smells, she'd gone all out for the return of her favorite grandchild. Brom found his father and brother in the living room discussing the ancient prophecy of the Silver Hunter. How he hated this topic. His hatred of the topic grew when he discovered the generations of magical breeding, which had already gone into the project. Now it looked as if prophecy was coming to pass in the person of his nephew, Kieran.

"Brom, there you are," his father said, looking up from a copy of the prophecy. "We were just discussing the development of Kieran's choice of boyfriends on the path of his journey toward becoming the Silver Hunter."

"Cory's inability to shift troubles us," Kellen said, directing his brother's attention to the page containing the prophecy. "He's supposed to have a shifter at his right and left side."

"Then maybe Kieran isn't the one destined to be the Silver Hunter, after all. Have you given him any time to grieve his sisters? The only reason Kieran's even in a position to become the Hunter of the House of Beauty is because they were all sacrificed to this prophecy. Hell, Kellen, have you even taken time to mourn your daughters or have you shut off your emotions?"

"How I grieve my daughters is none of your business, Brom. Kieran has to be my focus. If he doesn't survive this, then everything for generations will have been for nothing. He's the last of the prime bloodline of the House of Beauty. None of the collateral branches will ever produce a candidate for the prophecy any time in the next twenty generations. A couple of Kieran's cousins are pregnant and might carry the Belle potential."

"You are so fucking cold, Kellen. You've lost five daughters and you haven't shed a tear for any of them because, like Dad, all you really care about is this cursed prophecy. This piece of insane ranting has driven this family for more generations than we can count. Take some time and become human again, little brother. Your son needs his father, not another slave driver. Dad has done enough of that over the years, never mind what the House of Beauty has done to him."

"Stay out of how I deal with my son."

"Why? So you can drive him insane with the damned prophecy? Let him live his life how he chooses and with the person he chooses."

"So I should stand back and let him take his beloved uncle's path and end up with his magic ruined because he didn't use a condom when getting fucked by a shifter with high traces of Ebony magic? No, Brother, I'm not letting Kieran fuck up his life like you did."

The argument was devolving into name-calling and cross accusations between the brothers when their father called it to an abrupt halt; he had spotted Kieran and a young blond man enter the room.

CHAPTER FOUR

Kieran and Cory arrived at the main house for dinner to find Kieran's father and uncle arguing in the living room. The energy in the room screamed of a long-running argument between the men. He noted that from the sound of things, they'd moved beyond whatever topic had started the argument into more personal and long-simmering disagreements. In a chair on the far side of the room sat an older version of both men, puffing on a pipe. He listened to both men argue without intervening until he spotted Kieran and Cory in the doorway. Kieran glanced at his grandfather and thought it odd that the man seemed to be enjoying the division between his sons. It was almost like watching Grandmother Belle holding court back at the House of Beauty. Kieran's blood ran cold at the thought of adding Cory to this mixture.

"Enough out of the both of you. My grandson and his boyfriend are here at my invitation. Behave yourselves or I'll send you both to your rooms without dinner."

"DAD!" two shocked voices rang out.

"If you're going to behave like you're both children, I'll treat you like you're children."

"I would give up now, Dad. Gramps always wins in the end," Kieran interjected, trying to draw attention away from Uncle Brom.

"This is between your uncle and I, Kieran, so mind your manners and introduce your boyfriend to your grandfather."

Kieran grabbed Cory's hand and dragged him across the room to stand before his grandfather. Cory glanced back over his shoulder at Kellen before he returned his gaze back to Kieran and his grandfather. Cory beheld the progression of how his lover would age over the years. Cory seemed impressed at how well the men of Kieran's family aged.

"Grandfather, this is Corwin Cooper, my boyfriend and partner. He's a member of a clan of shifters trying to breed the curse out of their lines, like the rumors we keep hearing. Cory, this is my grandfather, Aodhfin Oisín."

"Meeting you is a pleasure, sir."

"So you're the little shifter who snagged my grandson's heart. Well, you're easy on the eyes. From the reading I get of your aura, you can't shift."

"Thank you, sir. No, I've never shifted in my life. My parents think I may be the first to break the family curse. Of course, they were a little disappointed when I came out as gay. I'm sure the pack and clan hoped I would help breed the next generation."

"Yes, I'm sure the news hit them hard. Kieran's coming out gave us a bit of a blow as well, but we love him beyond measure. As long as you're good to my grandson, you're welcome in my home."

"I promise to always be good to him, sir."

A rich female voice called from the next room. "If you boys are done yelling and inspecting the merchandise, dinner is served. Come eat before all my hard work gets cold."

Kieran led Cory into the family dinning room where a table groaned under the weight of the food placed upon the surface. They found each place setting marked with name cards, and the boys found themselves seated next to each other opposite Kellen and Brom with Kieran's grandparents seated at the head and foot of the table. Kieran caught the beautiful silver-haired lady by the apron strings and wrapped her in a bear hug before she escaped into the kitchen.

"Kieran Samuel Belle Oisín let me go this instant. I still need to put food on the table."

"Honestly, Grams, if you put any more food on the table, the thing will collapse under the weight. I want you to meet someone special to me first."

Kieran turned them around to face Cory, who couldn't hide the grin on his face at the interplay between Kieran and his grandmother. He introduced Cory to his grandmother, Líadáin. After the formalities of introductions wrapped up, the family sat down to dinner. The tension between his father and uncle resonated in the room, leaving Kieran to wonder what might be causing problems between them. He decided on cornering his uncle after dinner to discover the problem. Decision made, Kieran turned his attention to his grandmother, and the two traded stories about the things going on in their lives.

Across the table from the boys, Kellen and Brom focused on their plates and on ignoring each other. They both resolved not to argue over dinner and ruin their mother's reunion with her favorite grandson. Líadáin came to Kieran's side when he came out as gay and there'd been no coming between them since. The kitchen became the first place to search when Kieran went missing from magic lessons with his grandfather. The boy's cooking nearly matched his grandmother's. Around the table, various dishes of familiar foods passed back and forth. Brom added helpings of his favorites to his plate while his thoughts turned darker and darker.

He opposed the plan to direct Kieran along the path to fulfill the ancient prophecy. The boy didn't choose to take the first steps along the path of prophecy when he took the test of the Tracker. Being born male in the House of Beauty dictated he serve as a tracker or servant. His gift from the Oisín side of his heritage made being a tracker inevitable. Step one down the path to prophecy. After running away to college, he returned home with a shifter for a lover and another for a guard dog. Step two and possibly three down the path. These supposed signs convinced his father and brother the events foretold in the prophecy might be coming to pass. They needed to make Kieran ready to face the predicted darkness. By opposing his family's plan, Brom hoped to give the boys a chance at a normal life. He must talk to the boys later and try to steer them off the path of prophecy. He focused back on the conversation going on between his father and Cory.

"My family would never attack you. We're trying to break the curse on our bloodline. Breaking the curse is one of the reasons Billy accepted the collar to stay in wolf form," Cory said.

Gramps' face flashed pale in shock before the crimson flush of anger began to spread across his face and his gray eyes began to flash silver at Cory's admission of the wolf in their party being another shifter. Kellen reached out to calm his father, even as he offered an explanation.

"The collar is Brom's work and Kieran's spell, Father. From what they told me of the boy, he loves his Uncle Cory and Uncle Kieran so much, he defied his grandparents and pack leader's order to choose human form and instead chose to become a wolf so he might stay with the boys."

The expression on Aodhfin's face warned Kieran and Kellen that further discussion would come and soon. Kieran took Cory's hand and held on tight. His grandmother dismissed them from the table, and Kieran dragged Cory out of the house.

"I think you made a mistake bringing us here, Kieran. Billy and I aren't going to fit into your family. We don't belong here."

"Of course you belong here. My grandmother is smitten; she loves you. You realize Dad approves of you, and I think you'll find Uncle Brom is on our side."

"I don't think your grandfather was thrilled when he learned Billy is a shifter locked in wolf form."

"Wolf, listen to me, you and Billy are my chosen family. Gramps will come around. I won't let anybody drive you and Billy away from me. Let's go back to the cabin and we'll curl up in front of the fireplace and cuddle."

"I guess I'm more tired than I thought. Let's shower and go to bed. Today proved to be a long day."

Taking Cory's hand, Kieran led them back to the guest cabin. Drawing his partner inside, Kieran took them to the huge downstairs bathroom, which contained a giant Jacuzzi tub. With practiced fingers, the dark-haired tracker made quick work of stripping down his blond lover. Kieran's fingers danced through the forest of dark blond chest hair traveling downward along Cory's treasure trail to the dense bush above his thick manhood. Lips and tongue soon followed fingers until Kieran knelt before his lover, tongue-flicking teasing licks across the tip of his lover's cock, bringing the beast to life. Before pleasure overwhelmed him, Cory pulled Kieran back to his feet and stripped him down so his smooth, lean body became exposed. By mutual agreement, they came together in a fierce kiss, which threatened to spark a fire. Lips moved along jawlines, seeking the pulse points along exposed necks, where tongues licked in sync to the heartbeats below. Hands explored as if for the first time they had touched each other's naked flesh. Cory made his way down his lover's smooth body to the right nipple, which he bathed with his tongue until the nipple became a firm peak capping the powerful pectoral muscle, before swiping across to render the same treatment to the left.

Kieran pulled Cory back up into a fiery lip lock as his hands roamed over his lover's firm back, moving down to his tight furry ass. Cory's hands found their way to cup and knead Kieran's smooth ass cheeks and to trace a finger down the valley between the cheeks. With a moan of pleasure, Kieran tried to focus enough to use his magic to start the tub filling as Cory's lips again moved over his throat and across his left shoulder. He experienced Cory's teeth brush against his collarbone. Would Cory try and bite him like wolves did when they mated? His lover's mouth moved back up along his neck and reclaimed his lips as his hands lifted Kieran by the ass and wrapped his lover's legs around his waist as he stepped over the edge of the tub and settled them both into the warm water.

Kieran reached back until his fingers found the controls to the jets and started the water bubbling around them. The change of position brought Cory's erection into contact with the valley of Kieran's ass, and the head slipped in to rub against Kieran's hole. Pleasure surged through both lovers as they embraced in the swirling waters. Kieran's fingers slid along Cory's neck, digging deep as they buried themselves in the thick blond hair. Cory's fingers played along Kieran's ass, teasing his rosebud along with the tip of his own cock before sliding up Kieran's back to tangle in the thick clump of Kieran's braided hair. The braid came loose under Cory's manipulation, spreading a dark curtain around the pair as they lost themselves in another soul-deep kiss. The jets of the tub shut down, and Kieran broke the kiss, rising and drawing his lover with him out of the tub. He grabbed a thick fluffy towel and began to dry Cory off.

When both of them dried off, Kieran led Cory naked through the cabin and upstairs to the loft, which held a huge king-sized bed. On the nightstand beside the bed gleaming in the moonlight coming in from the skylight was a bottle of lube and several condom packages. While the boys practiced monogamy, they agreed to practice safe sex until they understood what each other's magic-tainted blood would do to the other. Kieran drew Cory down on top of him, and the two resumed their interrupted lovemaking. To the world outside their bedroom, their relationship would seem as if Kieran was the dominate in the relationship, but in the bedroom, Kieran let go of all his take-charge persona and let Cory be in control. They didn't define their roles in lovemaking; Kieran didn't always bottom and Cory didn't always top. Often, Cory led Kieran into topping him so they remained equals in their relationship. Tonight, Cory kept full control, and after prepping Kieran, he took him for the ride of his life. When they were spent, Cory cleaned them up, snuggled up behind Kieran, and wrapped him in his arms as they drifted off into sleep.

CHAPTER FIVE

For the first couple of days during their visit to the Oisín compound, Kieran and Cory relaxed and explored the forests around their cabin, dined with the family in the evenings, and returned to their cabin to make love. During the family dinners, Uncle Brom would drop hints as to the project he was working on, hoping to entice Kieran to come out to the forge and work with him again. Gramps still brooded over Cory's welcome to the compound and remained distant from the boys.

On their second Saturday at his grandfather's estate, Kieran couldn't contain his curiosity any longer and dragged Cory along with him to Uncle Brom's cabin and forge located on the opposite side of the compound from the boys' cabin. Drawing closer to the clearing, they detected the sounds of tools hammering on metal and inhaled the scent of burning coals. Brom stood over an anvil, hammering out a length of iron into the rough shape of a highland dirk.

"UNCLE BROM!" Kieran screamed so his uncle would be aware of him over the din of his work.

Brom turned and smiled at his nephew and his boyfriend. Cory contemplated the scene before him as Brom grabbed a towel to wipe away the sweat from his naked torso and his face. As he moved, his muscles rippled under his skin. Where Kieran was smooth, Brom had a thick mat of dark hair across his pectorals, thinning to a trail down the center of his abs to the top of his jeans. The family resemblance between Kieran and his uncle seemed to be the face and the silver eyes. Cory shook himself when he realized he was staring at his boyfriend's uncle like a prospective date or trick. He blushed when he caught Kieran watching his reaction to Brom. Kieran merely smiled at him, which never failed to melt his heart.

Kieran leaned into Cory's side and whispered into his ear, "He affected me the same way once, Wolf. One of the reasons why I love all your fur."

Cory blushed harder and Kieran laughed.

"So what is this mystery project you wanted my ideas on, Uncle Brom?" Kieran asked to direct his uncle's attention away from Cory.

"Well, the principle is based on the collar we designed for Billy. I'm trying to figure a way to change the spells enough to allow such a design to be used against hostile shifters. Adaptive spell-shaping isn't my strong suit," Brom confessed.

"I don't suppose another collar like the one we made for Billy or my notes are laying around any place handy?" Kieran asked, looking around.

"Check the middle drawer of the drafting table. I think I put your notes in the drawer after I forged the collar and the spells."

Cory, standing closer to the drafting table, pulled open the drawer only to leap back, shaking his fingers from the sting of Silver magic. Kieran moved quickly to his side, drawing the Silver magic out of his lover's hand.

"Sorry, Cory. I forgot to warn you about the ward," Kieran said before kissing each fingertip.

"I should realize something important like designs would be warded with magic."

"Yeah, Wolf. This might not be a comfortable place for you between the heat and the magic."

"I can tolerate the heat and I need to build up a tolerance for your magic. We won't always have time for me to get to some distant place so I can avoid your magic."

"All right, but if the magic gets to be too much, head back to our cabin and I'll find you in the bedroom when I'm done here." Kieran drew Cory in for a deep kiss and unbuttoned his lover's shirt to expose his furry, sweat-slicked chest. "You're going to melt if you keep this shirt all buttoned up." Kieran's actions reminded his lover of the heat pouring off the forge.

Cory flushed from both the heat and desire for a moment before yanking Kieran's t-shirt over his head, leaving his lover bare to the waist. To add a bit of a tease, Cory used Kieran's shirt to wipe the sweat from his own chest before tucking the tee into his back pocket. Kieran's face took on an indignant expression for a moment before laughing and returning with the notes to work with his uncle. Cory regarded the two shirtless men as they put their heads together to study the notes regarding the collar and how to change the magic from voluntary to involuntary. The magical technical talk and the heat finally began to bore Cory, so he wandered off and found a quiet spot down by a creek, which flowed past Brom's clearing. He sat on the bank and took off his shoes and socks before dangling his feet in the cool water. He pulled Kieran's tee out of his pocket, took off his own shirt, and folded them together into a pillow as he lay back on the bank to study the clouds through the tree canopy. The mix scent of his and Kieran's sweat on the shirts invaded his senses as he let himself drift, and soon, his cock got hard in his jeans. Cory reached down, stroked himself through the dense fabric of the jeans, and grew harder. He repositioned himself in his jeans, undid his belt, and pulled down the zipper to expose his bulging boxer-briefs. The fabric grew damp from sweat and pre-cum. Cory found himself glad he wore a colored pair of underwear because a white pair would be transparent from the moisture. His left hand tucked up under his head exposed his hairy pit and the curve of farm labor toned muscle; his right hand stroked down his furry chest to the waistband of his boxer briefs and over the bulge of his thick full cock to cup his balls. Cory drifted in self-pleasure as his hips rose. His hand slipped his jeans and his briefs down below his balls before rising to stroke the turgid length of his cock with a lazy, teasing stroke. His fantasy thoughts started out with slowly undressing Kieran, kissing and licking his exposed skin, slowly running his fingers through Kieran's hair while he nibbled and sucked on one of his tender nipples. Running his tongue across the firm and furry pectorals to the other nipple before following the treasure trail down to where the folded leather apron lay still wrapped around the trim waist. Hearing Brom's deep voice as the man moaned his name in pleasure.

Cory sat bolt upright, all the pleasurable thoughts vanishing from his mind as he found Kieran transforming into Uncle Brom in his fantasy. Even worse, he realizes Brom's deep voice was actually calling out to him.

"Hey, Cory, come on back to the cabin. Kieran and I are going to take a break for lunch." Brom's voice echoed through the woods.

Dressing quickly, Cory headed back toward Brom's cabin and lunch with his boyfriend and the man in his sudden fantasy. He was worried Kieran would sense his thoughts had strayed to another man. Cory thought to himself, *In some ways, I'm as naive about sex as Kieran is. I never made love to anyone older than I am, so I guess I dreamed about what having a more experienced partner would be like.* He arrived back at the forge and Brom's cabin to find Kieran sitting alone on the front stairs with a couple of cold bottles of water at hand. Cory didn't like the expression of concern on Kieran's face as he glanced up at his lover. He hoped the expression was something to do with the spells for the collar and not anything that bled through the deep bond they shared. Kieran handed him one of the bottles of water and patted the section of stair beside him for Cory to sit.

"I think we need to talk, Cory, because I'm surprised you didn't come back when I called for you."

Cory bowed his head and nodded, while his hands destroyed the label on the water bottle.

"You realize I love you deeply and truly, Wolf. This bond between us is new to both of us, and because I deal with magic all the time in my life, I experience things more intensely than you do. I shared your pleasure and your intense feelings of guilt. I don't understand what caused the sudden shift in emotions."

"I was daydreaming about making slow love to you, but for some reason, your body became your uncle's. I don't understand why, other than he's as beautiful as you are but in a more mature way. I love you with everything in my heart. I don't get why thoughts of your uncle invaded my daydreams of you."

"Okay, I admit I didn't expect you to be replacing me so quickly in your sexy daydreams. I'm guessing Uncle Brom turns you on because he's older and more experienced than I am. I suppose being in love with someone who was a virgin when you met them is hot for a while, but you miss sex with someone with maturity and experience."

The sad expression on Kieran's face tore Cory apart. He set down his water bottle and took his lover's face in his hands, lifting his chin so they looked each other in the eye.

"Kieran, I don't care about experience. I care about love, not sudden bouts of lust. I'm sorry for being human in such a way. You said yourself your uncle is sexy. You're the one I love, and to me, you're the only person who matters. I can't promise my eyes won't wander, but you possess my heart and my heart will never stray."

"I hope not, Cory. I gave you my heart and soul. If I lost you now, life wouldn't be worth living. I guess I can't hold your fantasy against you if you want to jack off to thoughts of what Uncle Brom would do to you in bed, but I hope I can blow fantasy away with the reality of me later."

"My love, you're better than any fantasy will ever be." Cory drew Kieran in tight and kissed him. "I think I'll go back to our cabin to get cleaned up and wait for you to come back to me when you're done here."

"You could at least stay for lunch, Cory. Uncle Brom should be bringing it out in a moment."

"I think we both need a little space to deal with my wandering mind. I'll grab something from the fridge back at the cabin." Cory kissed Kieran one more time, got up, and walked back across the compound to the cabin where he and Kieran were staying. Kieran stayed seated on the steps of his uncle's cabin, waiting for the older man to come out with lunch.

****

Brom on his way out to the porch overheard Kieran's conversation with Cory and the part about his abrupt appearance as Cory's fantasy lover, and Brom's heart ached for Kieran and how mature he sounded as Cory tried to apologize and patch things up between them. He waited until Cory left before making noise as he juggled the plates of sandwiches through the screen door of his cabin.

"Hey, give me a hand here or the ants will get lunch instead of us," Brom called out.

Kieran grabbed the plates and set them down on a nearby table before grabbing his uncle around the waist in a fierce hug and letting go of his grip on his emotions. Sobs wracked the younger man as tears soaked his uncle's shirt. Wrapping his arms around his sobbing nephew, Brom's heart shattered anew at the pain, which struck so close to home. He stroked Kieran's back and let the boy sob himself out. He didn't cry like this. Not since his mother's funeral. When Kellen brought him here, as far as Brom recalled, Kieran lost control and cried.

Kieran settled against his uncle, seeking the comfort only the older man gave him. Kieran didn't let his emotions control him and he never let them get the better of him, not even in private. Brom ushered the boy over to the rustic couch with its overstuffed cushion on the porch and settled them both down. Kieran curled up against his uncle, as he'd done when he was a little boy needing comfort or whispering secrets he couldn't tell his father.

He never revealed the causes of his heartaches to anyone other than his beloved Uncle Brom.

"All right, *mo stór*, tell me what's tearing you up like this. I can tell when you're bottling things up again."

"I'm glad you still think of me as a treasure, Uncle Brom. I experience times when I think you're the only one who does despite all the protestations of how much I'm loved around here. There's tension in the air that's never been here when I've visited before. You and Dad are fighting over something I think has to do with me, because you stop when I enter the room. Even Gramps is acting odd. I get the feeling he and Dad are hiding some ulterior motive behind everything they do of late."

"Not true, *mo stór*, they love you as much as I do, and trust me on this, if your grams didn't love you more than she loves her own children, she would never teach you how to cook her most secret recipes. As for your father and I, let's just say I don't like the fact that he hasn't stopped to mourn your sisters or given you time to mourn them either. So what's bothering you?"

"I'm worried I don't possess Cory's heart, like he says I do. While he was off in the woods, the pleasurable experience he gave himself resonated through our bond, but when he broke off, I got this intense flash of guilt overriding everything. When he came back, it was after you called out instead of when I called him, as if he didn't hear my voice. He had this guilty expression on his face, and he confessed to having an erotic dream, which started off with him making love to me but ended up with him in bed with you instead." Kieran blurted out the last part of his admission before hiding his face against his uncle's chest.

"Well, his confession is a shocker, and I confess I overheard his apologies to you for having a wandering eye. I didn't realize I'm the source of his distraction. What he finds in a old guy like me is beyond me."

"He discovered how hot and sexy you are," Kieran mumbled against his uncle's chest.

"Something tells me, *mo stór*, someone else experienced a crush on me."

Kieran merely nodded against his uncle's chest. Fear sent shudders through Kieran's body before he sat up and put a little distance between himself and his uncle.

"I couldn't help crushing on you. I was ten. You are the first male to show any concern for me besides Dad. You were a strange man who opened his heart as well as his arms to a broken little boy, who lost his mother. I fell in love with you the moment you wrapped me in your arms and called me *mo stór* for the first time. Dad broke the spell by introducing you as his brother and my uncle. I was crushed to discover all the fantasies about growing up to marry you couldn't happen between blood relatives. Best and worst five minutes of my childhood."

Brom chuckled at the flush of color on Kieran's face at his admission of his juvenile crush on his own uncle. Brom realized male role models were seriously lacking in Kieran's life, as was male-male affection. He took Kieran's left hand and studied the ring intensely. He noted the wolf's head representing Kieran appeared a bit smaller than the one depicting Cory. The dynamic seemed odd with Kieran being the beta of the relationship; from everything Brom witnessed, Kieran was more an Alpha personality and seemed to lead Cory around. This might be part of the problem. Kieran didn't yet realize his position in the relationship and tried to stay Cory's equal. Brom made a mental note regarding the rings seeming a little loose, which meant one of their hearts strayed, and he figured the wandering heart belonged to Cory's, given the details of the boy's confession to Kieran.

"What should I do, Uncle Brom? I don't want to lose Cory, because deep down, we are made to be together, but what if all this is infatuation and not real love?"

"I can tell you this is real love, *mo stór*. You crafted the magic of those rings, so it wouldn't work for anything less. You need to talk with Cory and find your footing. I think your spells worked better than you realized. Take a close study of your ring. Do you realize the wolf representing Cory is slightly larger than the one that represents you?"

"I never realized the size difference before. I always thought they appeared equal in size. This means Cory and I aren't equals, and he should be the Alpha in our relationship."

"Yes, *mo stór*. Be careful. Until we can test his blood, raw sex with a shifter might damage your magic and put you in danger when you undergo the initiation to become your father's and grandfather's heir to the power of the Silver Witch."

"I want a normal life, free of magic and shifters. I don't want to be the legend some stupid destiny is trying to make me. Besides, I don't recall any tales with the hero or legend as the submissive half of a relationship."

"I think you might be surprised at how the dynamic works, Kieran. The hero goes out, does all heroic stuff, and comes home to someone who reminds them they're only human after all."

"I guess you make sense. I promised Cory I would always protect him. How do I be protective and let him be the dominate in our relationship? He doesn't possess magic, he can't shift, and the people who seem to want to hurt us can do both. How does an almost-normal guy protect a tracker and witch like me?"

"You need to talk to Cory about how to handle any situation which arises, *mo stór*. Now eat your sandwich before the ants discover free food."

Kieran ate the sandwiches Brom put on his plate. He put away more food than either of them expected him to consume. After they finished eating; uncle and nephew sat in companionable silence for a while. Kieran rose and excused himself.

"I think I better get back to our cabin and talk with Cory. We need to talk before either Gramps or Dad shows up to start the initiation process. Thanks for listening, Uncle Brom."

"I'm always here for you, *mo stór*."

Kieran dashed off for his own cabin to find Cory and talk. Shortly after he left Brom's cabin, Kellen arrived at his brother's place. The brothers settled in on chairs on the porch for what Brom realized was going to be a long discussion about his nephew and Kieran's boyfriend.

INTERLUDE: UNCLE BROM DRAWN INTO THE FAMILY PLOT

Kellen settled in on his brother's porch and sighed because what he needed to ask of his brother would put them at odds over Kieran and Cory. The brothers sat in growing silence before Brom finally spoke.

"All right, Brother, what are you and Dad cooking up to do to my nephew and his boyfriend?"

"We need to keep them separated for about a week so I can initiate Kieran and test his limits."

"Kellen, you do realize they're bonded. Those rings on their left hands are ones I forged to Kieran's specifications. I don't think even Kieran realizes the adaptive power of his spells. Understand this, Brother, as long as their bond lasts, those rings won't come off."

"I understand better than you realize, Brom. What I need you to do is to help us block their bond so they can't experience what's happening to the other."

"No, Kellen. They're having a rough enough time of things already. I won't add to their problems. Cory isn't sensitive to the bond like Kieran is. The boy doesn't possess magic, and since he's not a full on shifter, he only experiences the connection on a primal level."

"What do you mean the boys are having a rough time already?" Kellen asked his brother.

"They were both here earlier today; in fact, you missed Kieran by a few minutes. Seems Cory's baser instincts got the better of him when he caught me all hot, sweaty, and shirtless working at the forge. He wandered off when Kieran and I got down to heavy magic talk and ended up out by the creek having erotic daydreams. Only problem is halfway through his hot dreams about Kieran, his mind took a sudden left turn and replaced Kieran with me. Passion turned to guilt, and Kieran sensed it all and confronted him about the daydream."

"I'm sure the conversation didn't go well."

"Actually, Kieran was mature about the whole situation, and Cory admitted the details without Kieran prodding him. He pledged undying love to Kieran but not faithful eyes, and I think he hurt Kieran more with his confession than with the fantasy. They need to work things out, and they do not need us mucking things up for them."

"I need to judge Kieran's limits without interference from Cory's shifter heritage. I need to determine if the shifter heritage he inherited from his mother's line is going to mess things up. If they're fucking without protection, Kieran's magic might be damaged or lost."

"I warned Kieran about the possibility of damage to his magic. He wants a normal life more than anything, Kellen."

"I get where he's coming from, but I'm afraid he can't. The Alpha in control of the pack on the Belle estate is a descendant of the damned Beast. Kieran is destined to be the Silver Hunter, or we're all lost."

"Sounds like you need to work on transforming Cory into an actual shifter instead of worrying about Kieran's magic. Doesn't your prophecy say something about a silver and ebony shifter on his left and right hand?"

"Yes, if you go by dad's translation of the prophecy, but silver shifters don't exist, so I'm guessing white is the proper translation of the passage, so unless Cory's animal form is a white wolf or something arctic, we're going to need to find a different shifter. Billy fulfills the ebony shifter."

"But the prophecy also said something about the white or silver shifter being the hunter's mate in one of the stanzas. I think you're stuck with Cory. I don't understand why you or father can't go and kill this Alpha. Either one of you is more power than any six silver mages."

"Because, like any other mage, we would never get through the forest of the Belle estate to confront this Alpha. The pack would tear us apart. Only Kieran possesses the skills to get to the heart of the forest and face down the Alpha. He's the only one with the proper bloodlines to do this, Brom."

"So are you asking me to block or break the connection between Kieran and Cory?"

"Break the bond if you can, but block the connection at the least."

"Go away now, Brother," Brom growled. "This power play makes me sick, but I will block the connection as best I can. Remember, Kieran is a more powerful silver mage than I am. He can break my spells with ease," Brom said as he stalked into his cabin and slammed the door behind him.

CHAPTER SIX

Kieran arrived back at the guest cabin to find Cory sitting on the front stairs in a pair of shorts and flip-flops. The sight of his boyfriend waiting for him made his heart skip a beat until he caught the expression on Cory's face. Cory was angry and his anger was directed at Kieran. Stopping short of the bottom stair, Kieran gazed up at Cory as the man stood.

"I was thinking while I waited for you to come back here. I shouldn't need to experience guilt over one stupid fantasy daydream. I'm not Mr. Perfect. I'm human. Therefore, my mind wandered while I was jacking off, big deal. I can't help your uncle is fucking hot, and yes, I do wonder what the experience would be like to be with someone older and more mature, Kieran. Every guy I ever dated was close to my own age or younger. So if my mind wanders from time to time, you're going to need to deal."

Kieran tried to keep the hurt from showing in his face and from flowing down the bond to Cory. He'd been all set to forget about the stupid fantasy and try to get their relationship back on track. Now, as he stood facing an angry Cory, he experienced the anger flowing down the link and feeding his own rising anger.

"Well, I guess all the crap about wolves mating for life is a lie after all. If you're so hot for Uncle Brom, go ahead and make a move. I'm sure he'll let you down as easy as he can. I guess I was the naïve little virgin, and now you get to add taking my virginity to your list of accomplishments, so I guess you're done with me. I should remember to never trust my heart to a shifter."

"Oh right, as if giving my heart to a fucking hunter wannabe was a brilliant idea. I moved my things to the downstairs bedroom for now. With luck, your father or uncle will be kind enough to take me to where I can catch the bus home to Arkansas."

"No need. You can take the van and drive your ass back to Arkansas, and take Billy with you. I'll leave my copy of the key on the island in the kitchen. Take the van. I won't need transportation."

"Oh, sure, and I won't be five minutes down the road before you call the cops and report the van stolen since the registration is in your name."

"The registration is in both our names, but I'll sign the title over to you as well. I'm done having my heart stomped on."

A flare of power surged through both boys' left hands as the rings on their fingers tightened with a painful squeeze before becoming loose and threatening to slip off.

"I would let this whole stupid incident go, Wolf. I do love you, but if you want to go, I won't hold you back," Kieran said, looking up with a mournful expression at his boyfriend.

Cory gazed down at Kieran, and for the first time, shared the true surge of emotions through their bond. Love, anguish, and loss slammed into him from Kieran, whom he realized was prepared to let him go if leaving was what Cory wanted.

"I love you too. I need time to cool down, and we can talk about this relationship with rational minds in the morning. I don't want us to be one of those couples, which argue and use sex to think they fixed everything. I'm going to sleep downstairs tonight so I can think."

"Fair enough. We can both think our relationship over and discuss where we go from here in the morning. If you want to leave, I won't stop you."

****

For the first time since their relationship reached the sleep together stage, Kieran and Cory went to separate bedrooms. They were both so depressed neither of them went up to the main house for dinner. A fact not missed by Grams, who asked pointed questions of her husband and sons at dinner.

"All right, you three, what's going on? Why aren't Kieran and Cory here for dinner?" Grams questions were sharp.

"The boys are having a bit of a relationship issue, and I'm sure they chose to stay at their cabin to work their problems out," Kellen replied before Brom said anything.

"What kind of relationship issue would keep either of those boys away from dinner?" Kellen noted his mother didn't let this topic go away.

"Kieran sensed a disturbance in their bond this afternoon while the boys were visiting me at the forge. When he asked Cory what was going on, Cory admitted to having a brief sexual fantasy, which started out with Kieran as the focus but somehow shifted to me being the focus. Cory's not as sensitive to the bond between them as Kieran is, so he couldn't tell how upset Kieran was about the whole thing," Brom confessed before Kellen interjected.

"I'm sure the boys will work this out and be fine by breakfast," Kellen said, trying to get his mother off the topic.

"But you would prefer they stayed apart until after Kieran's been tested and you discover if he can inherit the power of the Silver Witch, Brother. I don't like your plan to disrupt their bond. They need the bond to find the proper balance in their relationship," Brom growled at his brother.

"I'm not going to sit back and let Kieran repeat your mistake. We can't wait for me to find a new wife and produce another son. Besides, no child I produce now would possess the proper bloodlines to become the Silver Hunter," Kellen retorted.

"I keep telling you to do your own dirty work. You want the dark shifter dead so badly, get old lady Belle to protect your ass while you make with the major magic," Brom shouted back at Kellen.

"Both of you be quiet. Camille Belle is too old and broken to act as Huntress anymore. If one of Kieran's sisters had lived to become Huntress, we might take the risk of doing this ourselves," Gramps interjected.

"But all the girls are dead and only Kieran is left of the direct bloodline of the House of Beauty. I don't like any plan which puts my grandson in harms way, and I forbid you all from messing with the boys' relationship. Let them work things out and figure where their relationship goes." Grams tone invited no further argument from any of the men at the table.

The Oisín Clan finished their dinner in silence.

CHAPTER SEVEN

After a nearly sleepless night, Kieran finally heaved himself out of bed and padded naked into the bathroom. After relieving himself, he stepped into the shower and realized how much he hated fighting with Cory as the water soaked his hair, forcing him to remember to use magic to get his hair clean and dry. *Cory loves taking the time to wash my hair, and I love the sensation of his hands stroking my hair and massaging my scalp.* With a frustrated growl, Kieran ran his fingers through his hair, letting Silver magic bind the dirt to his hands before releasing the magic under the spray of the shower. When he stepped out of the shower, he bound the moisture in his hair to the towel. He returned to the bedroom and donned a pair of shorts before grabbing a plain leather band, which he used to bind his hair into a loose ponytail. Padding barefoot downstairs, Kieran headed for the kitchen. Soon, the aroma of coffee filled the air while Kieran began rummaging in the fridge for ingredients to turn into breakfast. With his ingredients assembled for stuffed omelets, Kieran set to work chopping ham, cheese, peppers, onions, and tomatoes into tiny cubes. After getting his *mise en place* assembled, Kieran set the kitchen table for two before turning his attention to cooking the bacon.

The rich aromas of coffee and frying bacon reached Cory's nose, and he gave up the pretense of trying to read the book he'd found on the nightstand in the spare bedroom. He padded barefoot down the hallway to the kitchen doorway where he stopped and studied Kieran move with the grace of a dancer as he tossed things in pans and made delicious scents fill the air. Kieran was so beautiful Cory couldn't understand why his eye had wandered to the man's uncle. Cory waited until Kieran set down the chef's knife and moved over to the sink to wash his hands before he approached. He slipped an arm around Kieran's waist and used his other hand to move Kieran's ponytail out of the way, so his hairy chest pressed against Kieran's smooth back as he pulled the man he loved against his body. Using his left hand, he found and captured Kieran's left hand and intertwined their fingers so their rings came together. A faint spark of power flashed as the rings touched, and he received an abrupt experience of Kieran's fear of losing his love and the deep sadness of the younger man.

Kieran broke the embrace and crossed to the stove to flip the bacon. He turned and faced Cory; for a moment, tears sparkled at the corner of his silver eyes. Open and vulnerable, his soul laid bare for a brief second before a stoic mask slammed down on his beautiful face. Cory's heart shattered at the pain he'd inflicted on Kieran. Worse was the knowledge he'd shattered Kieran's trust in him. Before Cory spoke anything further, Kieran raised his hand and placed his index finger on Cory's lips to stop him from speaking.

"No, I don't want any more apologies, no matter how sincere they are. I want you to take a good hard glance at the wolves on your ring and study the sizes carefully."

Cory raised his left hand and stared at the silver ring with the two wolves heads, one with amber eyes representing him and the other with diamond eyes representing Kieran. The inspection took him a few moments to discover Kieran's wolf was slightly smaller than his own wolf. He raised his head to peer at Kieran as he realized he was meant to be Kieran's protector and Alpha to Kieran's beta. When Kieran sensed the understanding dawn on Cory's face, he sank to his knees and tilted his head up and to the side, barring his neck in submission. Cory sank to his knees opposite Kieran and reached out to raise Kieran's head back to a normal position.

"Babe, I'm honored by your submission, but I hurt you and broke your trust in me. I don't deserve your submission at this time. When I earn back your trust, I'll claim my Alpha rights."

"Wolf, by admitting you're not worthy to claim your rights as a pack Alpha instead of taking them as is an Alpha's due, you proved I can still trust you. I want you to claim me totally as your mate. I don't care if mating damages my magic."

"No, I won't ruin your magic. Surely we can find a way for us to complete the mating without hurting you or your magic."

"I remember hearing of two ways which might protect my magic, but I don't think either Dad or Gramps will go for them. Uncle Brom might help, but he's not strong enough anymore to do this alone."

"What are these ways, Kieran?"

"We bind my powers so I can no longer use them, sort of like we bound Billy to one form. The other is a ceremony, which strips my powers from me for a time. This ceremony is used to seal a committed relationship. The problem is they both require a Silver mage more powerful than I am, which means only Dad or Gramps are able to perform the ritual for us."

"So we need a way to get them to use their magic without knowing they're binding your powers. What if your uncle crafted some piece of jewelry and got them to cast the power-binding spell on the piece?"

"I'm sure he would, but the spell is specific to the magic being bound, and they'll wonder why he wants to bind a Silver mage more powerful than he is."

"I don't understand all the workings of magic, but sometimes Dad uses a talisman when he needs to cast a spell on himself, yet retain the ability to break the spell. What if you use me in the spell like a talisman so you're able to cast the magic yourself, remembering I can break the spell if we need your powers back?"

"I'll need to do some research on this one."

"Let's begin your research after breakfast. I think you're going to need a do-over on the bacon. From the aroma, you went beyond extra crispy."

"Ugh, I'm a better cook than this, honestly."

Kieran got up off the floor and quickly took the smoking pan of incinerated bacon off the stove and dumped the ruined pan in the sink. He found another pan, while Cory poured two cups of coffee and prepared them how he and Kieran both enjoyed it. He placed Kieran's on the counter beside the stove and took his own over to the table. After rearranging the settings, placing them next to each other, he sat down to study his lover as he cooked. Cory let his love for Kieran flow through him, hoping his lover would sense the emotion through the bond they now shared. Kieran smiled at him with one of his billion-watt smiles, and this one reached his lover's eyes, making them sparkle. Getting playful, Cory focused on an image of Kieran naked on his knees with Cory's cock buried to the pubes in his throat. Kieran moaned, his cock going rigid and tenting his shorts as he flushed red all over. Cory teased Kieran further with a thought of him on his back with his legs up on Cory's shoulders as his lover teased his hole with the tip of his hard cock. The moan from Kieran got deeper and more need-filled than before as his flush deepened, and a wet spot began to form on his shorts near the head of his cock. The click of the burner being shut off was the only warning Cory got before he found himself on the floor with his shorts vanishing with a tingle, which told him of Silver magic's involvement, before a warm wet heat wrapped around the head of his cock. Kieran swallowed his lover's cock to the root on the first go. Now came Cory's turn to moan in intense pleasure. Kieran worked Cory's cock with tongue, throat, and mouth until his lover struggled to draw a proper breath. The abrupt stop left Cory teetering on the brink of orgasm. Kieran rose and smirked at his prostrate lover. Cory's quick recovery and his reaction caught Kieran off guard as he turned back to try to make breakfast. Kieran found himself on his back with a naked Cory pinning him down and a raging hard-on staring him in the face. Cory snarled in his sexy lust-filled voice.

"You don't get to walk away with the job unfinished, lover. Now open wide and get your hot mouth back on my cock."

Kieran whimpered in submission and swallowed Cory's cock to the root, once again taking his lover to the edge, but this time, Cory kept him from stopping, taking control of the blow job and transformed the service into a skull fuck until he blew a huge load down Kieran's throat. Kieran swallowed and kept going until Cory pulled free as his cock reached a level of sensitivity even he couldn't take. Cory stretched himself full length on top of Kieran and nuzzled his lover's neck at the join to the shoulder where he bit down hard enough to bruise. Kieran moaned and turned to expose more of his neck in wolf-like submission, letting Cory lick and nibble leaving his scent all over Kieran.

"Mine," Cory growled in Kieran's ear.

"Yours," Kieran whimpered as he nuzzled back.

Cory got up and scooped Kieran from the floor, carrying him up to the main bedroom where their supplies were. Once in the bedroom, he made short work of stripping off Kieran's shorts before tossing his lover on the bed. Kieran bounced once before Cory pounced on him and pinned him to the mattress. Kieran moaned as Cory's tongue went to work on his body, erasing all traces of Kieran's own scent before Cory smothered him with his body, coating him in Cory's musky scent. Cory flipped Kieran over and repeated the process on his lover's backside. After making sure Kieran was covered in his scent, Cory slid down and began to rim and tease open his lover's ass, getting him loosened up for a deep mating fuck. Before long, Kieran was a moaning puddle of jelly from the rim job.

Reaching over to the nightstand, Cory grabbed the lube and a condom package settled in to suit up. He ran a lubed finger over Kieran's twitching hole and lightly teased into his lover's body before shifting his position to let the head of his thick heavy cock rest on and tease his lover's entrance. Whimpers from beneath him drove his now actively dominant nature to sink into the tight warmth of his lover's body, claiming him as mate. Slow and gentle quickly transformed into hard and fast as Cory's love and lust collided with and was influenced by Kieran's through their bond. At the height of passion, as they were cresting toward mutual orgasm, Cory once again bit down on Kieran's shoulder with bruising force, triggering their mutual explosive orgasm. Cory collapsed on top of Kieran panting as his cock was milked dry by the spasms of Kieran's ass muscles. When they both came down from the world-rocking orgasm, Cory reached down and grabbed a hold of his condom to keep the thing from slipping off as he withdrew. Even for a second orgasm in a short period, his load bloated the end of the condom. He tied the condom off and dropped the used item in the trash. He rolled over on his back and pulled Kieran in tight so his lover was pressed into his side with his head on Cory's chest. Kieran, for his part, snuggled in and drifted in satisfied contentment, inhaling his lover's scent. They drifted off to sleep wrapped in each other's arms.

****

Kieran and Cory woke late in the afternoon but stayed cuddled in bed for a long time, enjoying being in each other's company. Finally, they decided to get up and shower together, even though Cory wanted to keep Kieran covered in his scent so others would recognize Kieran was his mate. Kieran rubbed against Cory letting him understand he would always be his. Once in the shower, Cory took to washing Kieran's hair properly, working the shampoo deep into Kieran's scalp and massaging down his neck before going to work on the rest of length. Kieran was purring like a cat as Cory worked on his hair. The task took awhile to get the length cleaned and the shampoo rinsed out, but Cory enjoyed every moment of his task almost as much as Kieran did. With Kieran's hair washed, Cory started in on washing his lover's body and realized the places where he'd bitten down on Kieran's shoulders didn't show the faintest trace of bruising.

"I'd expected to find my bite marks on your shoulders. You should be sporting a couple of huge hickeys on you considering how hard I bit down on you."

"Only by breaking the skin would you leave a mark, Wolf. Remember, I heal fast, and surface bruises fade fast. I love how you tried to mark me as yours, Wolf. I am yours, so you don't need to worry about marking me."

"I want others to recognize you're mine. I'm in a serious wolf-like state of late almost as if my beast were moving closer to the surface."

Kieran turned in concern and gazed deep into Cory's amber eyes, which brought a surge of the beast up in Cory until Kieran dropped his gaze in submission and offered his throat.

"Sorry, I don't understand where this is coming from," Cory said as he licked along Kieran's throat from shoulder to earlobe, making Kieran shudder.

"Your beast is closer to the surface, Wolf. I'm beginning to suspect your inability to shift isn't from sudden miraculous breeding by your parents. I think someone bound your ability with magic and the binding spell is breaking down."

"Do you think Dad did something after my birth?"

"He would be my first guess. Silver magic isn't binding you or you would have been in incredible pain all your life. I think we'll quietly ask Grams to scan you after dinner tonight, and if the binding is Sapphire magic, she can fix—or at least strengthen—the spell."

"I don't want to shift."

"I don't want you to shift either, Wolf. We're tied into the stupid prophecy enough. I want a long and normal life, not a short legendary one."

The lovers got out of the shower, dried off, and returned to the bedroom to get dressed for dinner with the rest of the family.

****

Kieran led Cory to the back of the main house and through a vast herb and vegetable garden to the door leading into the kitchen. He wanted Grams to check Cory over before they ran into any of the other Oisín family members. Both boys sniffed deeply of the heavenly scents coming from the kitchen door as they entered.

"Wipe your feet and wash your hands, boys. I have work for both of you," Grams said as she placed a bowl of potatoes fresh from the garden on the work island in the center of the kitchen.

"Yes, Grams," both young men replied as they complied with her directions.

When they finished washing their hands and taken a place at the workstation, Grams placed a bowl of water, a scrub brush, and an empty bowl in front of each of them. The bowl of potatoes between them, Kieran sighed knowing they're tasked to clean the potatoes. Grams' philosophy, *idle hands get young men in trouble*, which she applied to Kieran at age ten when he came and stayed with his father's family until things settled down on the Belle estate after his mother's death.

She did her part to keep young Kieran out of trouble. Líadáin taught him how to work a magic she guaranteed would win him the person of his dreams. Kieran learned to cook, use herbs, and set a proper table. He returned to the Belle estate less rebellious and with a purpose once again.

His goal firm in his mind, he managed to convince Grandmother Belle to let him spend every other summer with his paternal family. The stern old woman permitted him two weeks to visit his father's family the summer he turned eleven as a reward for his performance during training. When he returned home with a beautiful handcrafted silver broach as a gift for her, she agreed to allow him to spend one month each summer with his father's family until he turned fifteen, and his training as a tracker for the House of Beauty began full time.

"Something serious is on your mind, *mo stór*, for you to sneak in the back way. The last time you did such a thing since you were twelve," Grams said, pulling Kieran from his memories. "So what brings you and *mac tíre óg* to my kitchen? You can both work while we talk."

Cory seemed puzzled by the Irish words, which he guessed meant Grams was talking about him. Kieran glanced at him and smiled.

"*Mac tíre óg*, means young wolf in Irish," Kieran said as he picked up the first potato and dunked the spud in the bowl of water before attacking the skin with the scrub brush. "Grams, Cory's wolf is getting closer to the surface, and we think his lack of shifting isn't due to genetics but rather a binding spell, which is breaking down."

"Why come to me, *mo stór*, and not your father or grandfather?" Grams said as she started chopping some herbs while giving Cory a glance, which made him blush and start cleaning potatoes.

"Because this binding isn't a Silver magic binding spell. The sensations are more akin to Sapphire, which means Cory's father

42

most likely, cast the binding. Since Sapphire magic is your talent, I figured we would be better off to coming to you. Besides, Gramps will get all upset about the barrier spell and go all end of the world on us."

"Well, the barrier spell needs to be taken into consideration, Kieran. The barrier keeps us protected from dark shifters and others who wish for Silver magic go the way of Gold and Amethyst."

"I understand, Grams. I keep waiting for Dad or Gramps to come and tell me my turn has come to add to the layers of the spell."

"Once you undergo the ritual to link you to the power of the Silver Witch, Kieran, you will take your turn adding to the layers of defensive magic in the barrier. Now, *mac tíre óg*, give me your hand, and let's discover what sort of interesting things I can learn about you." Grams reached across the worktable to take Cory's right hand.

Kieran tried to focus on cleaning potatoes as his grandmother's magic washed over Cory, searching out the spell, which bound his shifter abilities. The room grew colder as Grams' magic worked and Cory's shiver was visible. Grams muttered words in Irish under her breath as she ended her scan of Cory. Kieran set aside the potato he'd finished peeling and stared at his grandmother in expectation.

"Don't stare, dear. Yes, *mo stór*, you were right to be worried. A binding spell of Sapphire magic is at work holding Cory's abilities as a shifter at bay, and the spell is breaking down because he's been ingesting Silver magic. I'm guessing you boys aren't using a condom when you perform oral sex on each other."

Kieran and Cory both blushed at the comment from Grams. She clucked her tongue in disapproval before continuing.

"The Sapphire magic of the spell is being eroded but at the same time is also working with the Silver magic to eliminate the Ebony magic in Cory's blood as well. He's balanced between the three types of magic."

"Grams, how does this relate to his beast being so close to the surface?"

"Had Cory's shifter genes not been blocked at an early age, his wolf would be dark, and yes, Cory, your animal form is definitely a wolf. I suspect not as dark as young Billy's wolf, since they don't share the same strain of the lineage. Your beast is fighting to stay dark, but the dark is losing the battle. The dark will lose for sure as long as you don't shift before the balance tips further toward Silver magic."

"Will I shift if the balance becomes more Silver magic than Ebony magic?" Cory was desperate for the answer.

"I can't say for sure, Cory. The shifter gene is a creation of Ebony magic. While some shifters possess traces of the other types of magic, no shifter ever possessed Silver magic."

"So if we tip the balance to Silver magic, I might never need to worry about shifting?"

"I can't promise, but if you keep the transition gradual as you're doing—even though you didn't realize what you were doing—I'd say your chances are good. You'll come as close to human as you will ever get. Be careful, you two." Grams moved around the worktable and drew both boys into a fierce hug. Kieran and Cory linked arms and held the woman fast between them.

"You'll never get dinner ready if you squash my wife between you boys," Gramps declared as he entered the kitchen.

Kieran and Cory let Grams go from their hug and scurried back to washing and peeling potatoes.

"Kieran, I need a word with you in private," Gramps called from the far side of the kitchen.

"Be right with you, Gramps," Kieran replied as he jumped off his stool and kissed Cory.

Kieran followed his Grandfather out into the herb garden and to a spot, which was reserved for Gramps to smoke his pipe. Grams hated the stink of the thing and had long ago forbidden him to smoke the pipe in the house. Gramps settled in his chair and Kieran sat on the ground, facing him as he'd done when he was much younger. He called this little corner of the gardens the wisdom patch, because here was where Gramps brought him when profound things were to be discussed. When they were both settled and Gramps had his pipe lit and drawing to his satisfaction, he gazed down at Kieran.

"Your father and I have been discussing your purification and initiation rituals, and we've decided I should be the one leading you through both."

"I'm honored, Grandfather. I always thought when the time came Dad would be the one who would be my guide for these rituals."

"Normally, Kellen would be acting in the role of guide and priest for these rituals. Family tradition plans for a father to initiate his son as his rightful heir to the power. We think you would be better served by becoming one of my direct heirs in case something happens to me."

This turn of events caught Kieran off guard. Worry crossed his expression. Might something be physically wrong with his grandfather?

"Gramps, what's wrong? Are you okay?"

"Oh, don't worry. My health is good, Kieran. I'm concerned these are dark times and so much of the ancient prophecy seems to be centering on you. I want to give you access to the full powers of the Silver Witch, not what you can draw on now or the slight bit more power you might get as your father's heir."

"Okay, Gramps. When do you want to do these rituals?"

"We'll do them next week. You must leave Cory behind. This is only for the Silver Witch and his heir."

"You do understand he's going to sense what's happening to me through our bond, Gramps. I can't take off this ring as long as he and I are truly bonded."

"Yes, Kieran. Your father will make sure Cory doesn't come looking for you or interfere with the rituals."

"Well, I'd better get back to helping Cory and Grams get things ready for dinner." Kieran rose and hugged his grandfather before heading back into the house. The idea of his father looking after Cory while he went with Gramps didn't sit well with Kieran. He decided as a precaution to ask Uncle Brom to keep an eye on Dad for him.

****

Dinner was a quiet affair without either his father arguing with Uncle Brom or Gramps debating with either of his sons. Kieran wondered what was up with his family. He sensed something off but couldn't figure what was wrong. When dinner finished, he led Cory out into the deep woods and along a hidden path to Uncle Brom's cabin. Letting themselves into the cabin was easy since Brom never locked the place. Kieran settled them down on the couch in the front room in what he thought of as their proper places. Cory leaned up against the arm, and Kieran snuggled in between Cory's legs, resting against his chest with Cory stroking his hair. They kicked their shoes off and got comfy on the couch as Uncle Brom came in through the

45

backdoor, yanked open the refrigerator, grabbed a beer (from the sounds of the clanking bottles), and stomped into the front room. He was startled for only a moment when he realized he wasn't alone in his own home and figured out who reclined on his couch.

"You boys surprise me. I figured I would be *persona non grata* around you two."

"We worked things out, Uncle Brom, and our bond is stronger than ever. Thank you for giving us the reason to make our bond stronger," Kieran replied.

"Well, this is a first. Actually, I expected your father to be here, *mo stór*. Instead, I find you two camped out like you own the place. Do either of you want a beer?"

"No, thank you, Uncle Brom. Kieran doesn't do well with beer and I don't drink." Cory's firm response came for the two of them. "What we want to understand is what's going on behind the scenes. Your father pulled Kieran aside earlier tonight to tell him something private, and everyone got so quiet at dinner tonight. The day has been kind of unnerving."

Brom scrutinized his nephew as the young man nodded along in agreement and snuggled in tighter to Cory, almost using the older boy as a shield. They accepted their bond and their roles within the bond. Kieran let Cory be the Alpha and take the lead.

"Did Kieran explain anything about the rituals he's going to be undergoing soon?"

Cory shook his head in the negative as his left hand caressed Kieran's hair; somehow never catching on the ring both boys wore. Kieran remained quiet; he wasn't allowed to speak about the rituals to an outsider. Brom glazed at him for a moment, silver eyes meeting silver eyes before he glanced up into the amber eyes of Kieran's lover. He witnessed the fierce source of protective strength in those amber eyes. He smiled at the boys, took a swig from his beer, and began a long explanation of purification and initiation rituals for Cory's benefit.

"So I can't be part of any of these rituals, but I'll experience everything done to Kieran through our bond, won't I?"

"Yes, Cory, you'll likely experience everything Kieran does. What worries me is the part of this where my father will invest Kieran with access to the power of the Silver Witch. If you absorb the magic through Kieran, the ritual may cause you harm because of the Ebony magic in your blood from your shifter heritage."

"Can I be shielded from any of this?" Cory asked.

"Tell me you recall a way, Uncle Brom." Kieran's eyes pleaded with his uncle as he spoke.

"You ever use the love displacement spell, Kieran?" Brom asked.

"Yes. Back when we first discovered how opposite our heritages are, I used the spell to hide my feelings away inside of Cory so I gained time to figure things out without my emotions getting in the way. Turns out the spell helped save me from some powerful dark force, which wants to enslave me."

"What you need to do is cast this spell again—only this time, draw your bond out of both of you and place the link someplace or into something safe until the rituals are complete. Removal of the bond is the only way to make sure neither of you will experience what's happening to the other until after you restore the bond," Brom said and hated himself for playing along with his father and brother and their plans.

"I'm not a fan of this idea. We can find some other way?" Cory asked Kieran.

"I might put a block on our bond, Wolf, but I'm not sure my block would hold against the power, which will flow along the channel and down the bond. Dad might be able to cast the spell, but I don't want to ask him to mess about with our bond. I can lock our bond into our rings, and you can hide the rings someplace safe until I come back from the rituals."

"Why don't you boys go home and discuss this further? Plans like this should be between the two of you," Brom said as he got out of his chair to encourage the boys to leave.

Kieran and Cory got up and put on their shoes before hugging Uncle Brom and heading back to their own cabin. Shortly after they left, Kellen came into the main room from the door leading to Brom's bedroom.

"I don't like how powerful their bond is, and I don't like seeing Kieran take second place to Cory."

"Kieran's role is partly the nature of their bond and partly due to his upbringing in the House of Beauty. All the strong men in his life—you, Dad, his uncles, and great-uncles on the Belle side—are like most of the women in his life, disciplinarians. Face the facts,

Brother. To survive in the House of Beauty, even you needed to become a doormat. Kieran loves and respects you, but he doesn't relate to you as someone who will comfort him when the world beats the crap out of him. I figured you realized why he comes to me when he needed answers and solutions to his questions and problems. I'm the guy he's free to talk and do fun things with."

"I hate when you're right. Old Lady Belle was hard on Kieran as a boy, his training was so rough, and all I did was keep the worst punishments from falling on him when he failed some task. I guess I was wishing he would come to me for advice like a son should come to his father."

"Oh please, how many times did you go to Dad for advice when we were kids, Kellen? Every time I turned around, you were running to Uncle Padraig for advice. Asking uncles for advice runs in the family, Kellen."

"Yes, I suppose so. So what will they do, come and ask me to block their bond or will Kieran cast the emotional removal spell?"

"I chose to send them back to their cabin to discuss what they want to do, so we wouldn't be forewarned. I want the boys to be happy. After almost wrecking their relationship, I don't want to be part of anything that drives them apart."

"I don't want them hurt either, Brom. I love Kieran with all my heart, and he's the last bit left of his mother. We need him more than you can imagine."

"I still say we should handle this shifter problem some other way."

I wish we only needed to deal with the shifter problem, but an Ebony mage is involved in this somewhere. If Kieran doesn't possess all the pieces to the prophecy and all the power we can give him, we're doomed."

"Okay, but one last question before you get as bad as Dad with the doom and gloom, little brother. What did the boys talk to Mother about before dinner tonight?"

"I didn't even realize they'd spoken with her."

"Well, you might want to find out before you muck about with their relationship too much. I only caught Mother mentioning something about a slow transformation process before I ducked out when Dad came toward the kitchen."

"You do understand Mother won't say anything to betray their confidence. We'll hope Dad's plan works and Kieran pulls their bonds out into their rings."

"You're planning to try and destroy their bond. Answer me this, little brother. Are you so sure Cory isn't the mate your precious prophecy talks about? Did you or Dad stop to think of a reason he never shifted? Sapphire magic can be used to bind as easily as Silver magic can."

"Sapphire magic wouldn't hold off the change of a born shifter. No Sapphire mage is powerful enough."

"What if the binding spell was layered over years and years of close contact? Stop and think, Kellen. You don't possess any information about Cory's family other than some of them are shifters. Talk to Mother before you ruin your son's life."

"I don't possess the time, Brom. I can only hope he'll forgive me," Kellen called back as he fled from Brom's cabin back to the main house.

CHAPTER EIGHT

Things were quiet around the compound for the rest of the boys' third week. Near the middle of their fourth week, Kieran exited the cabin to find his grandfather standing in the clearing in front of him. He was dressed in what Kieran had come to think of as training clothes, sturdy leather boots, pants, and shirt. At Aodhfin's side were silver hiking staff, a travel pack, and large leather-bound book. Kieran took all this in with a quick glance before turning around and retracing his steps into the cabin to change into his own training gear. He also explained to Cory their plans for the day had been changed by Aodhfin's desire to start training with Kieran again. Kieran changed from his jeans and t-shirt into his leather tracking clothes, including the heavy leather duster. On his hips, he wore the matching pair of silver Hungarian sabers; twin silver daggers poked their hilts from the tops of his boots. Kieran kissed Cory with all the intensity of their love for each other and the promise to be back as soon as he possible before he left the cabin and joined his grandfather.

Aodhfin took up his hiking staff, the book, and his pack, leading Kieran off into the woods while Cory's eyes followed their departure from the porch with Billy sitting at his side. In silence, Kieran followed his grandfather into the forest for hours until they arrived in a clearing he didn't recall being to before. In the center of the clearing stood an altar-like table on top of which was a bookstand. Aodhfin placed the large book he'd been carrying on the stand before facing Kieran. Grandfather and grandson stared at each other for a long moment before Kieran knelt before his grandfather without a word being spoken.

"Tonight we will begin your initiation into the ranks of the Silver Witches of the House of Oisín. You will be consecrated to the ancestors, after which will begin your training to become the Silver Witch and assume command of the grimoire our family has spent centuries crafting. First, you must be cleansed in the scared springs; strip and leave your clothes and your modesty behind as you follow the path laid out by our ancestors."

Kieran rose and stripped, leaving a pile of clothes, weapons, and silver chains behind him as he padded barefoot across the clearing to the pathway leading to the sacred springs. His grandfather beheld how Kieran had developed in body and had a flash of pride pass through him as his grandson passed naked before him. He hoped his grandson would forgive them for what they planned to do to Cory while Kieran was undergoing the purification ritual. Aodhfin went and tidied up Kieran's pile of clothes, weapons, and silver chains before taking a different path down to the sacred springs. He espied the double-headed wolf ring lay on top of the pile. Aodhfin's path led to a special alcove, which housed the herbs and oils needed to begin the cleansing ceremony. Here, Aodhfin stripped away his clothes and weapons, donned a white loincloth and a silver pendant, which marked him as the Silver Witch before continuing to the springs.

When Kieran arrived at the sacred springs, he stood on a stone overlooking the three pools. The pool to the left was a hot spring, which appeared to lie directly above its heat source as the water steamed and nearly bubbled with the heat. The pool to the right seemed to be a cold pool; the stone edge appeared to be rimmed with ice despite the heat of the season. The central pool lay below both of the others, and here, their waters mixed to a perfect temperature. In front of this pool, Aodhfin stood wearing only a pendant and a loincloth; behind him on a table about waist-high rested several towels and sacred oils. Kieran made his approach and knelt before his grandfather, a supplicant before the font of purification.

"These pools are sacred unto the goddess of the moon and her consort the god of the sun. What seek you here?"

"I come seeking purification before undertaking an important quest for knowledge and power to be used in the defense of mankind."

"What knowledge and power do you seek, O mortal youth?"

"I seek the knowledge of my ancestors and the power of the Silver Witch."

"You seek much, O mortal youth. By what right do you seek such knowledge?"

"By my descent from the last woman to hold the power of the Silver Witch, she who was mother to both my mother's line and my father's line. I claim the heritage of both the House of Beauty who slew the Beast and of the House of Oisín."

"Step into the pool until you are submerged to rinse away all earthly impurities."

Following the instructions, Kieran stepped into the pool and sank below the surface. His hair spread out as the small current in the pool swirled around him—first hot, then switching to cold—before enfolding him in a comfortable warmth like the fluid of the womb. Slowly he rose to the surface as the pool raised him up on a platform of Silver magic and allowed him to step off on to the ledge where his grandfather stood, face now hidden behind a silver mask with no features. The mask was a silver mirror to Kieran, but its magic allowed Aodhfin a clear view of everything from within. Aodhfin pointed to the table, and Kieran lay down on the surface face up, hair streaming down a trough behind his head. He closed his eyes as Aodhfin placed a white cloth over his face. Aodhfin, now in the full role of high priest to the goddess, took up the sacred oils and began a massage of consecration starting from his grandson's feet and working upwards to his neck, skipping over his grandson's hardening cock and tightening balls for the moment. He chanted the special prayers to open both his grandson and himself up to the powers of the goddess and to the Silver magic.

Power rose along his spine, flowing back and forth, as his grandfather's hands worked across his body until the power began to pool in the lowest of the ancient power points in his groin. Kieran experienced both the power and an orgasm building in his manhood. Would his own grandfather bring him to physical orgasm or was something else intended to release the power and his seed? From behind the veil of fabric covering his face, Kieran sensed a power rising outside of his body in the place where his grandfather stood and realized his grandfather was transformed by the presence of the goddess' consort the god. Now the divine spirit made use of the earthly flesh to keep the ritual pure and removed from the taint of incest. The god took hold of Kieran's cock, and with three sacred strokes, brought forth an orgasm of both magic and physical seed, which left Kieran drained and sore.

"Your sacrifice is accepted and banked against the needs of your sacred line, Kieran of the Oisín and the Belle."

The power vanished from the grove, and Kieran found himself on the edge of blacking out as he sensed his grandfather slump down next to him. After a time, Kieran stirred as he listened to his grandfather moving about the area. He opened his eyes to find himself lying on a sleeping bag in the first clearing. Sitting up slowly,

Kieran examined the scene and found his grandfather had started a fire, and he sniffed food cooking. The sound of a stomach growling announced Kieran's recovery to Aodhfin who handed his grandson a plate of bread with honey smeared on the slices.

Even chewing slowly and washing the bread down with spring water, the plate was empty in mere moments. Kieran experienced some of his strength flowing back into balance with food in his system again.

"I don't recall ever being this off balance from a cleansing ritual before, Gramps."

"This was the most powerful one you will ever be involved in, Kieran. We only used this version when the Silver Witch dedicates his successor."

"I sort of tingle as if I'm a live wire, while also being as empty as a drained battery."

"The live wire sensation is your newly opened channel to our ancestors' magic, and the dead battery sensation is your personal power, which drained away when you reached orgasm during the ritual. The first will fade into the background in a day or two, and your personal power should return after a good night's sleep."

"When all this training is done and the rituals are completed, am I only going to be one of your successors, Gramps?"

"Yes, Kieran, but you possess access to many of the powers of the Silver Witch, but in truth, you will still only be my successor as your father is still only my successor."

"So the full powers of the Silver Witch still belong to you?"

"Yes, only the death of the Silver Witch or a deliberate severing of the power will transfer to his successor the full powers of our family line. Only one Silver Witch at a time is the way of our family since Beauty's brother became the first male Silver Witch following their mother's death. Get some rest now, boy. You'll get more family history as we continue your training."

Kieran settled back into the sleeping bag to get some sleep. He tossed and turned in the bag for a while before sleep final overcame him. He'd learned early last week he didn't sleep well alone anymore; he was used to Cory's solid form wrapped around him.

CHAPTER NINE

When Kieran went with is grandfather, Cory had been left to his own devices to entertain himself and Billy. His wolf-shaped nephew was content after going for a brief walk to settle down on the porch of the cabin and sleep. Cory made his way up to the main house in his wanderings where Kieran's father met him. Kellen wanted all the details of how he'd met Kieran and about his own family and clan. Cory spent the better part of the day reliving his relationship with Kieran for his lover's father. Grams brought them food and drink, while Kellen poured on the questions, probing for details about the Cooper family's quest to purge the shifter blood from their line, Billy's birth, and choice to become a wolf instead of a boy and dozens more.

Finally, Grams took pity on him, and after packing him a late night snack, he sent him back to the guest cottage. Cory put his snack away for later and made sure Billy had water and food in his bowls before climbing the stairs to the loft. If the cabin seemed empty without Kieran to share the place with, their bed seemed even more so. Cory cuddled Kieran's pillow to himself, seeking the scent of his lover to ease him into sleep. A fitful night's sleep finally overtook Cory until a dream dragged him under.

In his dream, Cory viewed from a distance Kieran stepping out of the trees onto a beach. Under the light of the full moon, the sand was silver. Cory beheld his lover in torn clothing, barefoot, breathing hard, and surveying his escape routes, looking to evade his pursuers.

His lover appeared worried as if something dangerous were pursuing him. Kieran's expression in the dream made Cory wonder what pursued his lover in his dreams.

Cory trembled in his sleep as in the dream he listened to brush crack behind Kieran, alerting him to the presence of his pursuers. Grabbing a stick, dream Kieran moved further out on the sand. He drew a circle around himself and waited. The direction of his eyes led Cory's dream vision to the edge of the forest, revealing at least six wolf shifters stalking him. The Alpha was a huge, dark gray beast, at least twice the size of the other wolves. Its eyes glowed bright yellow in the moonlight, and its vicious canines flashed silver. The beast prowled forward with the rest of its pack close on its flanks. Cory followed the events in fear as the beast scented Kieran and let loose a fierce howl of victory. Kieran braced himself, and silver began to flow along the length of the stick down to the circle around him. The Alpha coiled and leapt at his prey, hoping to drag Kieran down so the rest of the pack can close in and help finish him off.

As silver flashed in a circle around Kieran, Cory blasted from the dream into a waking state by an instinct telling him he's not alone in the bedroom. He rolled from the bed ahead of sword blade slicing down where he'd been a moment before. From the shadows on the far side of the room, Kieran's father emerged with a long and deadly silver sword. Cory sprung to his feet, racing for the stairs, ignoring his own nudity. He grabbed Billy by the silver collar to keep him from charging up the stairs to confront the mad man with the sword.

"Tonight is a full moon wolf-boy. Shift and fight me."

"I can't shift. Are you forgetting I don't possess enough shifter blood to make the change possible? What will Kieran do when he finds out you're attacking me, Kellen? You're his father. How can you betray him like this? If you hurt me, Kieran will never forgive you, and he'll never do what you want him to do."

"You must be tested to determine if you're truly worthy to be my son's partner."

"Tested? I would give my life to protect Kieran. You're mad if you think attacking me will cause me to abandon Kieran." Cory backed up a few steps looking for something to use as a weapon. Beside him, Billy growled defensively.

Kellen charged swinging his sword like the mad man Cory named him. Billy and Cory barely escaped its path. Cory grabbed the table lamp and swung the lamp like a club at Kellen. Turning to make another pass at the pair, Kellen found he was blocked as another figure ran in room wielding a heavy silver broadsword. Short dark hair and a heavier frame revealed the man to be Kieran's uncle.

"Stop, Kellen. The boy proved himself to my satisfaction. He stood his ground and refused to let the beast attack you."

"So now you want me to spare Kieran's pets? Get out of the way, big brother."

"I had a vision while I was working at the forge, Kellen. The boy will help Kieran along the path destiny chose for him to walk. Kieran and Cory possess the potential to be truly mated, because unlike our line, the House of Beauty carries the contamination of shifter blood."

"Impossible, they're bred to hate and to hunt shifters? When did they ever mate with one?"

"According to my vision, Beauty herself is the source of the contamination entering the bloodline. Her idiot prince and the Beast shared a mother who was half-shifter. Their mother's blood is what makes Beauty's descendants such good trackers and hunters. The prince's shifter blood gives them heightened senses and speed."

"So why can't Kieran shift?" Cory asked

"Beauty's daughter used her gift of the Silver magic to bind the shifter genes in such a way no child of the house would ever be able to shift. Cory, this is something you must never tell Kieran."

"Oh, goddess, what do I do now? Brom, Dad doesn't possess any of this information, does he?"

"Now we wait to find out how young Kieran fares in the tests to become the next Silver Witch. We should go so Cory can get some rest."

Brom led his brother from the guest cabin, bidding Cory good night. Cory led Billy upstairs, put on some sleep pants in case of any more surprise visitors, settled into the bed, and let the wolf spend the night in the bedroom. *I wish we didn't strip away our bond, I need to be sure Kieran is all right and to be sure he's aware I'm all right as well. I wish the removal spell didn't work. If the spell failed, Kieran would be here by my side instead of out in the woods somewhere.*

CHAPTER TEN

Kieran and Aodhfin spent several days out in the forest engaged in training both magical and physical. Aodhfin focused a lot of the lessons on breaking the habits Kieran had developed from his training with his mother and the senior trackers of the House of Beauty. Kieran had a disturbing tendency to rely on physical tricks instead of letting his magic flow in the open. Aodhfin blamed Kellen for some of Kieran's lack of freedom with magic. Kellen helped train the boy to hide his power from his mother's family, in part to keep the Oisín hidden. The natural inclination of the House of Oisín was to keep hidden from the rest of the world to protect the most powerful of all the binding spells ever cast.

Aodhfin was impressed by Kieran's creative streak at using his magic as an extension of some other act.

"Kieran cast the spell and forget about masking the magic. You won't be able to mask the more powerful spells in the family grimoire." At Kieran's puzzled expression, Aodhfin said, "Yes, I understand I'm contradicting everything your father taught you."

Kieran pulled himself up short from the maneuver he'd started and let the magic flow. He scrutinized the spell while the magic took form and fizzled. He took a stance and attempted to cast the spell again without trying to disguise what he was doing. Again, the spell took form and fell apart. After several more attempts to cast the spell without hiding its form, Kieran stood frustrated.

"Plain casting doesn't work, Gramps. I don't think straightforward casting is how my version of the Silver magic works. If I'm going to become the Hunter of the House of Beauty, I'm going to be casting in combat. I won't get the time to stop and cast a spell."

"You're going to learn the proper forms of spell casting, Kieran. Learning the proper forms will be on you. The burden is yours. You must prove to me you can cast the most powerful spells from the grimoire in the traditional manner."

"The way to go about this is to skip over the spells I cast on a regular basis and go to spells I'm not familiar with. I need to learn spells which aren't combat focused."

"Well, put away your weapons and come over here. We'll start with a simple locator spell and focus on a target you're acquainted with. I think young Cory will hold your focus."

"I think you're cheating, Gramps. With the rituals over, all I need to do is put my ring back on and I'll find where Cory is through our mating bond. Hey, do you recall where I put my ring, Gramps?"

"You mean this ring?" Aodhfin said, holding up Kieran's bond ring.

"Yes, my bond ring," Kieran, said as he crossed to take the ring from his grandfather.

"This bond must end. Someone like Cory isn't meant to be at your side, and he certainly shouldn't be in your bed. Prophecy says you must take a shifter as your mate. We will find you a female shifter, so you can produce children to continue Beauty's line."

Kieran's expression turned to horror at his grandfather's words and outright shock when his bond ring twisted and melted in his grandfather's hand before vanishing. His grandfather stood stock-still for a moment, as if listening to a far away voice.

"According to the message spell I received from your father, your Cory is still alive. Apparently, Brom had some sort of vision at the forge last night and stopped your father from completing his task. Your father is upset and confused now. Seems your shifter put up a good defense before Brom stepped in. I guess I can let you keep him as friend."

Kieran's horror and shock turned into anger at his grandfather's betrayal.

"What gives you the right to get between Cory and I? I'm supposed to be around to protect him. I gave him my word I'd always protect him. Now you tell me I not only failed to protect him, but I failed to do what I promised from someone in my own family. I would expect this crap from my mother's family, but I never for the life of me figured you would pull this on me, Gramps. Wipe away your sense of smug satisfaction about destroying my bond to Cory, Gramps. You are not the only one who can plot against family when the need arises. You cannot understand what life is like for a child of the House of Beauty. So, while I cast the emotion separation spell, I didn't lock the bond into our rings."

Kieran crossed the clearing to his weapons and gear, quickly packing them up so he could get back to Cory and Billy. As he grabbed up his coat, his grandfather's magic grabbed his arm. Kieran exploded in fury at the binding spell and shattered the spell without a thought. Anger turning his beautiful face into an ugly mask of rage,

Kieran whirled on his grandfather, a magic blade blazing in his hand. Aodhfin took a step back from his grandson and raised both hands in a warding off gesture.

Slinging his pack over his shoulder, Kieran turned and left the clearing, heading back to the guest cabin. As soon as he was far enough away from the clearing, he took off at a run. He raced back to the cabin so he might find Cory and find out what had happened. He crashed into the front room to find Cory sitting in front of the fireplace talking with his grandmother. When Cory spotted Kieran, he launched himself across the room, his fist catching Kieran in the jaw. Kieran staggered backward. After the first fist, Cory's entire body crashed into him. His lover's anger at him rode down the mating bond from Cory's ring, shattering the spell along with Cory's ring. When the spell shattered, it returned to Kieran all the feelings of their connection. Cory's anger flowed through him and joined with his own fury. In his confused state of intense rage, Kieran's magic surged between them, sending Cory flying across the room with a scream of combined rage and agony.

Both young men regained their feet with near inhuman speed. Before they raced at each other to clash in close quarters again, a wall of sapphire ice formed between them.

"Stop this at once, both of you," Kieran's grams said as she thickened the ice between the enraged lovers. "You two are the last ones who should be at each other's throat."

"Where were you when your insane father tried to kill me? I poured my fear and love into the bond to call you back. You promised me I would break the spell if I pushed hard enough. You promised me I'd be safe here with your family despite my heritage. You promised me by our bond, Kieran."

"I did, and I failed you. Only now has the spell broken. I didn't figure they'd try to kill you while the bond was suspended. We discussed what we thought were the ways needed to protect you from the amount of Silver magic pouring through me. Neither of us considered a physical attack on you into our plans. I love you more than anything, and I would never let them harm you. I don't even have my ring to prove how unbreakable our bond is to you. Gramps destroyed the symbol of our bond. I love you, Wolf."

Before Kieran dropped to his knees in submission, Cory stopped him.

"Go away, Kieran. I can't deal with you now. I don't understand how the mating bond chose so wrong when instinct picked you for my mate."

Cory turned his back on Kieran, refusing to meet his lover's anguished face. He raged at Kieran for failing his promise, and his words cut Kieran to his emotional quick. Spell or no spell, Kieran failed to protect him from Kellen's madness. *No,* a voice in his head screamed, *you're the one who should be protecting him; you are the Alpha of this relationship. You're the one who is supposed to be guarding Kieran's heart.* He sensed Kieran's emotions as he turned and fled the cabin. Cory understood the pain he inflicted on his mate. A voice like ice cut him from across the room.

"Those last words were totally uncalled for, young man. My grandson loves you with every fiber of his being. Do not blame him for something, which is not his fault. The training to become the heir of the Silver Witch is intense. You would do well to find him and forgive him before he does something you'll both regret."

"He promised me he would always be around to protect me. When I needed him most, he wasn't here. How do you forgive so many broken promises?"

"Don't blame my grandson for the actions of his elders. You're the Alpha in your relationship; you should be protecting yourself and Kieran, not expecting him to come running to your rescue. These are dangerous times, Cory, and I'm sorry, but Kieran is the focal point. You are either his strongest support or his Achilles' heel. Only you can decide where you stand. I suggest you take back those hateful words."

Turning, Cory found the ice barrier gone, so he raced from the cabin with Billy on his heels as the wolf came as if sensing his need. Billy passed Cory and sniffed the air before setting off along a path deep into the forest. Cory followed, hoping to find his love before Kieran found time to inflict deep wounds of self-loathing on himself. What seemed like hours later, Cory and Billy found Kieran sitting on the bank of a clear pool at the base of a small waterfall. He sat, stripped down to his boxer briefs, and his hair was wet. Despite the breaking of branches beneath Cory's feet, Kieran didn't move until Cory touched him on the shoulder. Kieran turned and buried his face in Cory's chest, wrapping his arms around his lover, and sobbed. The sorrow Kieran experienced washed down the mating bond and into

Cory like a flashflood. Wordlessly, he enfolded Kieran in his arms and in his heart, letting his love wash away the words said in anger and fear. As the agony of heartbreak and failure was replaced by the joy of love and acceptance, the lovers found themselves stretched out in the soft grass along the pool's bank. Kieran rested his head on Cory's chest and let his hands wander his lover's body.

"I'm sorry I said what I did back at the cabin. Mating bonds don't ever choose wrong, and I don't need a magic ring to prove how much you love me."

"I guess not needing a ring is a good thing since both of them are gone. Wolf, what I still can't understand is how your mating bond would have chosen me in the first place. I'm a descendant of two of the most pure mage lines in existence. My bloodline contains not a drop of shifter blood."

"Listen, bloodlines aren't important now. What's important is we're together and we need to find a way to keep anyone from breaking us apart again. If you want a consolation prize, Uncle Brom is pissed at your grandfather for getting your father to attack me."

"You're trying to make me forgive Dad for attacking you, aren't you, Wolf?"

"I guess I am a little. He is your father, after all. No point in ruining your relationship with him."

"Thanks. I'll talk to him. I promise. For now, I want to enjoy us and let our love wash over us both."

"We can do better. Make love to me and let your love wash through me, and let's purge the last of the Ebony magic from my blood."

"If we do this, Wolf, we will change the dynamics of our relationship. Are you sure you want me to be Alpha?"

"Yes, make love to me and forget the condom. I want you to be the true Alpha in our relationship. Since you swore to protect me, I want to be your true mate and submit to you in all ways."

"Wolf, this trust is special, and I'm afraid. I realize everyone seems to think I should be the Alpha in our relationship, but I actually relish giving you control. If anyone should be submitting, I think I should be the one. I'm still worried about what might happen when our opposing magic collides. I want our true mating to take place someplace special. Forgive me for asking for a little time to set things up to make for a night we'll never forget."

"Kieran, you realize I'll wait for you forever. I'm glad you trust me enough to give up control, but I think we can do this and still keep our balanced relationship. Understand this, Kieran Samuel Belle Oisín, I'm not letting you out of my sight until after we've truly mated and nothing will ever block us from knowing when the other needs us."

The lovers cuddled together for a while longer before Kieran rose, stripped off his still damp briefs, and pulled on his other clothes. He pulled Cory to his feet, and with a sharp whistle, called Billy in from his romp in the forest. He led the way back to their cabin where they cleaned up and got ready for dinner at the main house with Kieran's family.

INTERLUDE: THE APPRENTICE AND THE MONSTER MEET IN SHADOW

A dark cloaked figure stepped out of the ancient forest into a clearing the reeked of death. Before him lay a pile of bodies, both human and wolf, in various stages of decay. The figure in the dark cloak made a gesture, and Ebony magic swirled around the clearing, speeding up the decomposition and leaving only bones. The magic gathered the bones and bound them into the form of a throne with a canopy of wolf skulls. The finials of the throne's arms formed from human skulls. The cloaked mage settled into the throne to await the arrival of the dark Alpha shifter who claimed descent from the legendary Beast.

Across the clearing, dozens of amber and green eyes reflected the light of the full moon as the shifter pack moved out of the tree line. In the middle of the pack strode a huge beast, half-man and half-wolf or bear. From the distance, the mage couldn't tell which, though he leaned toward bear. *Well, seems the legendary claims of this Alpha shifter regarding his ancestry were true.* Only a shifter with a dark and powerful lineage would be able to hold the midway form of a shift. To be both beast and man during the full moon took incredible power no lesser line possessed. The pack stopped a distance from the enthroned figure while the Alpha continued forward to stop a few feet from the throne. Definitely a bear—a grizzly from the appearance and size of the Alpha—surprising given the pack was all wolf-shifters. The mage and the monster stared at each other for a moment longer before the shifter spoke.

"You are late, shifter."

"Do you bring me word of the boy who would be a hunter?"

"He and his boy toy along with the cur managed to lose my agents somewhere in Virginia. The boy took an assignment from a local hunter who turned out to be more talented in Emerald magic than she appeared. She masked the boy's trail from my agents."

"Why are you here?"

"I am here because my Master discovered the boy made his way here to Maine. Powerful spells now keep them hidden. Most likely he is hidden away by his bitch of a Huntress grandmother."

"The boy did not return to the House of Beauty. If he came here, we would not be meeting."

"So sure you can kill the boy like you did his sisters. He's not like any of his sisters. You won't spook him into wasting his magic."

"He's a male of the House of Beauty; he doesn't possess magic of his own. He will die faster than his sisters. The middle one made a formidable Huntress; pity she failed to survive our trap. Go now and find the boy. Beauty's accursed bloodline must end so the spell may be broken and shifters may be free."

CHAPTER ELEVEN

After sending a note the previous evening to the main house advising the rest of the family they wanted to take time for themselves, Kieran, Cory, and Billy went for a hike the next morning. They stepped out into the glade on the near side of a creek. Kieran carried a picnic basket his grandmother packed and left on their porch, a blanket thrown over one shoulder and his camera bag over the other shoulder. The boys and their wolf settled down near the creek, spread the blanket, and set down the picnic basket. Unslinging the camera bag from his shoulder, Kieran surveyed the glade and found a couple of spots he wanted to use as background for photos of Cory and Billy.

The young men and the wolf settled down to eat their picnic and enjoy the peace and quiet of the deep forest. Kieran's grandmother packed all kinds of food in the basket for the boys and the young wolf. Kieran shook his head as Cory and he pulled out enough food to feed ten people. They tucked in until they were full and couldn't eat anymore; then, they repacked the basket. Cory resettled the blanket near the base of one of the old growth trees near the creek and sat with his legs in front of his and his back against the tree. Kieran settled on his back with his head in Cory's lap, while Billy flopped down in the grass between the boys and the creek.

The lovers rested in each other's presence, enjoying being normal. Cory ran his fingers through Kieran's silky dark hair and let them play lightly over his lover's face, almost as if he tried to memorize Kieran's features like a blind person learning their sighted friend's facial structures. His fingers eventually trailed down Kieran's neck and under his shirt collar to the scars on his lover's chest. Cory's fingers eventually wandered across Kieran's chest to find one of his nipples and tweak the nub playfully. Kieran reached up and pulled Cory down into a tongue-filled kiss. They shifted to lay side by side on the blanket to continue kissing and touching each other with ease. Their kisses deepened, and they became so lost in each other they didn't sense the arrival of Kieran's grandfather from the opposite direction. The first indication of Aodhfin's attack came from Billy's yip of pain as Aodhfin zapped him with a cantrip. Kieran reacted fast. Cory found himself flat on his back as Kieran surged to his feet; Silver magic flaring to turn the creek into a barrier. Aodhfin's found his counter spell deflected and himself swept off his feet as Kieran bounded over the creek and tackled him. A gleaming silver dagger appeared against Aodhfin's throat.

After making his point, Kieran got off his grandfather and helped the older man back to his feet. As he turned to cross back to Cory, his grandfather's power wrapped around his chest and pinned his arms to his side. Rage surged as his eyes followed Aodhfin across the creek headed toward Cory and Billy, a silver staff materializing in his hand. Fury powered Kieran's reaction, and his grandfather's binding spell shattered as silver armor formed, and Kieran vaulted the creek powered by Silver magic to land between Aodhfin and Cory. Scythe-like blades ran from both elbows to a similar distance beyond Kieran's wrists. Silver magic swirled around both grandfather and grandson as they faced off. As grandfather and grandson glared at each other over weapons, another voice rang across the clearing.

"So this is how you decided to continue with the testing, Father? We all realize the enemy won't give the boys a chance to rest and be happy if given the opening, but aren't you pushing things a bit hard?" Kellen said.

Before Aodhfin or Kellen might react, they found themselves flung across the clearing and each of them bound to a tree. Kellen actually experienced his own power draining away from him and flowing into Kieran.

"If you think for even a moment I'm letting either of you get anywhere near Cory or Billy again, you're dead wrong. If you ever come anywhere near them with a weapon or magic raised to harm, the fact you're my blood family won't matter. I will kill you. They are my family as much as you are, and for the remainder of our stay and the rest of these tests, they are off-limits."

Kieran released his father and his grandfather and dropped the barrier across creek. As he was turning to face Cory, he caught movement out of the corner of his eye as Kellen charged him with his long sword raised for a deadly strike. Kieran spun and set himself into a defensive position with one deadly scythe blade ready to block and the other held back for a counter attack. Kellen swung with all his strength behind the weight of the blade. Kieran blocked the attack and directed his father's sword along the edge of his own weapon, but didn't follow through with his own counter attack; instead, he lashed out with a powerful kick to the back of his father's legs. Kellen staggered from the blow, but recovered and was quick to strike back at Kieran. For his part, Kieran blocked with his weapons beating back the long sword between the two scythes. With magic powering his strength, he forced his father back toward the stream, their blades still locked together. While Kieran seemed distracted, Aodhfin leapt over the creek and went for Kieran's exposed flank. Surprise caught Aodhfin as a heavy branch swung by Cory intercepted the heavy staff. Billy launched himself at Aodhfin's legs, trying to bring the man down. The contest brought Kieran and Cory back to back against Kieran's father and grandfather with Billy snapping at both older men from outside the combat. Kieran shoved his father back, disengaging their weapons. Off-balance, Kellen fell backward into the creek with his long sword sinking deep in the earth. With Kellen out of the fight, Kieran whirled to find Cory managing to hold off Aodhfin's attacks with his branch. When Cory slipped and fell, Kieran leapt over his lover and caught his grandfather's staff in the X formed by his crossed weapons. Knowing he was off-balance, Kieran dropped to one knee, still trapping his grandfather's staff between his own scythe blades. With an unknown strength, Kieran shoved his grandfather's heavy staff up and out, and lunged into the older man with a shoulder, driving the air from the man's lungs. Aodhfin landed on the ground, gasping for air as a single scythe blade stopped short of his throat.

"Give up, both of you, and stay down. You may have taught me magic, but Mother and her family taught me to fight in real combat. Neither of you are skilled fighters, nor are your hearts in the fight, while we're fighting to defend someone we care about. This battle is over, you two."

Kieran let his own Silver magic fade away, releasing his armor and his father at the same time. The power he'd taken from his father flowed back, leaving him weak. Cory was by his side as he started to sag from the energy drain. Billy placed himself between the boys and the older men as Kellen rose from the creek and came to help his father. Cory helped Kieran back to the blanket they'd laid out and got him seated with a bottle of water. He glared over his shoulder at Kieran's father and grandfather before deciding to ignore both of the older men and focus his attentions on his lover. He handed Kieran a second bottle of water when he found the one in Kieran's hand empty. He rummaged in the picnic basket and found some bread left over from their lunch. Kieran shook his head at the bread before leaning back against the tree and closing his eyes. Kieran stirred only when he made out his father lifting his grandfather to take the man from the clearing.

"No more tests, Gramps. I think we all understand what I did here today. Tomorrow, I'm taking Cory down to the beach, and we're camping for a week. When we get back, you both need to be ready to do whatever rituals are needed to make me the next heir to the Silver Witch."

"I'll make the arrangements, and we'll be ready when you boys get back," Kellen replied.

Aodhfin and Kellen put away their weapons and limped away from the glade. Cory snuggled in next to Kieran on the blanket and hugged his lover tight. Kieran lightly stroked his hand down Cory's side and held his lover.

"This next week is for us, Wolf. We're going to hide away from the world and make love to each other and complete the mating bond when the time is right."

INTERLUDE: THE PROFESSOR AND A HUNTER SPEAK ON THE PHONE

The renegade hunter, Alex Kincaid, sat in a booth at the back of a seedy dive bar in Boston's South End, trying to drink away his troubles. No matter how hard he tried to get close to the Belle kid, something kept blocking him. First, the hunter, Richard St. Martin, warned the kid off from working with him. The next interference came from the damned Emerald witch and her disruption spell throwing him off Belle and his cur of a boyfriend's track. So here he sat, drinking and trying to figure out how to find Belle so he might deliver the kid to the crazy Professor Simms. He took his time getting hammered, and his frustration grew at a rate where any little thing would set him off. Kincaid pounded back his whiskey and slammed back his beer. Before he signaled the waitress for another round, his phone rang.

"Kincaid."

"Did you find the boy yet?"

"You're aware I didn't fucking find the boy yet. If I did, he would be lying naked at your feet."

"I suggest you get out of the seedy bar you're in, sober up, and get back on his trail."

"His fucking trail is a month cold, thanks to the fucking Emerald bitch."

"She's been dealt with, so sober up, and start hunting him again. The compass in your possession will find him now. The witch who cast the disruption spell is dead."

"Hope you're right this time, cause if I need to find him without magic, I can't promise he'll be in pristine condition."

Kincaid's whiskey glass burst into flames and went out fast.

"A reminder, Mr. Kincaid, I can reach you anywhere."

"Fuck you, Professor Simms! You're easy to find as well. Don't threaten me with your parlor tricks. I'll deliver the Belle kid to you. Make sure my money is ready." Kincaid hung up and jammed his phone back in his coat pocket.

Now he was pissed. Taking orders from a mage rankled Kincaid. The wimpy professor giving him his marching orders would never be the kind to get his own hands dirty.

Like hell, I'll show the fucking pansy ass mage how a hunter finds his prey. Kincaid slapped enough bills down on the table to cover his bar bill and leave a tip for the waitress who kept his glasses full without him having to signal her. Calm, clear thinking is what he needed to be doing, if he planned to hunt a trained tracker such as Kieran Belle.

Rough, hardcore sex always served to calm him down. He could imagine the male prostitute as the professor as he fucked and beat him until he achieved orgasm.

CHAPTER TWELVE

To regain his strength, Kieran took a day longer than he thought he would need after his confrontation with his father and uncle. Cory did his best to spoil him by bringing food up to their bed and feeding Kieran in between rounds of kissing and snuggling, among other things. Once his strength came back, he rummaged around the cabin for the supplies they needed for their stay down at the beach. Kieran packed everything into two backpacks, and by the afternoon, the young men got on their way to the beach part of the Oisín compound. Before they left, Kieran took both his own and Cory's cellphones and put them on the night stand by their bed in the cabin. Billy trotted along and roamed off into the woods along the path to chase the local wildlife.

After walking for a couple of hours, the sound of the surf pounding reached their ears, and they soon reached a point on the path overlooking the coast. Kieran stopped to let Cory take in the view of the ocean waves crashing into the rocky coast. The sea spray reflected rainbows as the water splashed off the cliffs. The white caps danced on the blue-green water of the inlet as the waves made their way toward shore. Cory stood entranced, watching the unfamiliar sight.

Kieran nudged his partner, and they resumed making their way to the place where they would spend the next week. The pathway wandered along the coastal cliffs at the edge of the forest and followed a gradual slope down to a secluded and sheltered sandy beach. When they arrived on the beach, Kieran set down his pack and helped Cory out of his. They took the tent from Kieran's pack and got the shelter set up. Kieran set up a fire ring of stones. Together, the lovers gathered wood from the forest at the edge of the beach and built a fire. While Kieran started getting things ready for dinner, Cory settled the rest of their equipment in the tent. He set up the sleeping bags as one big bag and settled the pillows on top of their packs. With their camp set up and dinner cooking, Cory settled in beside Kieran on a blanket, watching as his boyfriend cooked over the open fire.

"You're a regular boy scout," Cory teased.

"Something of the sort at least, Wolf. I've been trained to survive in the wilderness by all my uncles. Uncle Brom taught me how to craft and use about anything as a weapon; my mother's brothers and my great-uncles taught me how to track, fight shifters, and how to recognize edible plants as well as how to trap, kill, and prepare wild game."

"The best I can do is push a cart around the grocery store if you want me to hunt down meat. I'm pretty handy in the garden though."

"I wouldn't expect anything less, farm boy. I think I would enjoy being a farmer's partner."

"I'm thinking I would be happy living a life on the coast."

"You would hate the winters up here. We measure the snow in feet, and the winter storms on the coast are fierce."

"I want to experience what winter is like up here. Do you think your grandparents would let us come for Christmas?"

"I'll ask them when I'm on speaking terms with Gramps again, but I warn you, this family celebrates the older traditions as well as the ones you're used to, Wolf."

"I don't care as long as we're making traditions of our own, Kieran."

"Cory, if I survive all the things I need to do this summer, you and I will build a lifetime of traditions. I promise you, we will live our own lives on our terms."

"Kieran, we survive the summer together or we die together. I want whatever time we have together to be lived to the fullest."

"We will live life to the max, Cory. Now let's eat. We're going to need our strength for all the lovemaking I have planned for tonight."

The young lovers ate to the sounds of the waves splashing against the shore and the hooting calls of owls in the woods. After they'd finished, Kieran sent Cory to the tent to grab a couple of towels from his pack while he cleaned up the dishes and banked the fire. When Cory returned, towels in hand, Kieran led him down toward the edge of the surf, drew him into a deep kiss, and slowly began to undress him. Cory started to move his hands to do the same to Kieran but was stopped when Kieran trapped his hands behind his back with his tangled t-shirt. Kieran kissed his way down Cory's throat and across his shoulder and back along the collarbone to the hollow of Cory's throat before working his way down Cory's chest to kiss and lave first the right nipple and across to the left one. Kieran sank to his knees as he worked his way down Cory's torso to his belly button where Kieran's tongue played in the hollow. Cory finally managed to free his hands from the tangle of his t-shirt as Kieran reached down and lifted Cory's left foot to remove both the sneaker and the sock. Cory used his newly freed hands to balance himself on Kieran's shoulders as his lover repeated his actions with the right foot. Now, Cory stood barefoot on the rough sand, clad only in his cargo shorts, and gazing down at his lover. Kieran surprised Cory by turning him around so he faced the sea as Kieran rose up behind him and held him tight, his arms wrapped around Cory's waist above his belt. Kieran rested his head on Cory's shoulder and took in the scents of his lover and the sea air for a few moments before his fingers unfastened Cory's belt and opened the fly on the cargo shorts. Kieran's hands quickly skimmed the shorts and the briefs beneath them off his lover, leaving Cory's body naked and gleaming in the moonlight. Cory turned around after stepping out of the shorts pooled around his ankles and slowly undressed Kieran with the same care and tenderness Kieran had showed him. When Kieran stood naked before him, Cory discerned how evident the scars across Kieran's chest became under the moonlight.

Cory made to speak, but Kieran silenced him with a kiss before leading him into the swirl of the sea. Cory shivered for a moment, unused to the cold waters of the Atlantic, but soon found warmth in Kieran's embrace. The lovers lost themselves in a kiss, which traveled to the depths of their souls.

Kieran's hands slid down Cory's body to cup his lover's ass and pull him in tight before pulling them both off balance and under the surface of the water. Cory broke free and surfaced, sputtering and spitting out salt water. He glanced around, looking for Kieran to surface, only to have his legs pulled out from under him by the still submerged Kieran. Cory crashed back into the water with a shout as Kieran surfaced between his legs. Kieran laughed as Cory rose up coughing up salt water and dove out of reach as his lover lunged for him. The two lovers dodged and splashed around in the surf until Cory finally snagged Kieran's braid and caught a finger in the chains, which held the braid together. He cursed as his finger bent backward before he pulled his finger free. Kieran caught his hand and kissed the injured finger before running his tongue across the palm of Cory's hand. He led Cory out of the water, where they scooped up their clothes before going back to the fire and settling on a log to dry off before crawling into their tent. Cory reached for Kieran's hair again but stopped at the top of the braid and gave Kieran a glance. Kieran grinned at Cory.

"I'll take the chains out of my hair and leave this mess loose for now. I have to do something with this mop or the length gets in the way. I should get my hair cut short and donate the braid to one of those charities, which makes wigs for cancer patients."

"As much as I believe in supporting charities, Kieran, don't you dare cut your hair."

Kieran reached up and popped the catch of the chains holding his braid together, and carefully slid the silver chains out of his midnight black hair. He ran his fingers through his hair and let his mane fan out over his back. The lovers settled into their sleeping bag and cuddled up for the night with Cory resting his head on Kieran's chest. Before long, they were asleep.

INTERLUDE: A WARNING, WHICH GOES UNHEARD

Richard St. Martin sat in the office of his antique store, listening to the message on Kieran Belle's voicemail.

"Hey, I'm busy and can't take your call now. Leave a message at the beep."

"Kieran, this is Richard St. Martin again. Word in the community is Alex Kincaid has been hired to hunt you down. He's already killed your witch contact in North Carolina, so don't rely on the cloaking spell she cast for you. Be careful. No one is sure where Kincaid is at the moment, and no one is sure how much magical help he has for backup." Richard disconnected the call and turned to figure sitting on the other side of his desk.

"Ambrose, I want Kincaid found before he finds Kieran Belle."

"And if finding Kincaid first isn't possible, Lord Hunter?"

"Rescue the boy and kill Kincaid, but do not turn him. I want the bastard dead."

"The task will be done as you command, Lord Hunter."

Richard St. Martin sank into his office chair once his right-hand vampire left the office. His own fangs elongated as his hunger at last overrode his control. Bright Goddess, how he hated his new existence. He called one of the many vampire sycophants from the former leader's court into his office. When the vampire entered, he was surprised to find an empty office, or so the room seemed. Richard pounced from behind the vampire and sank his fangs into the poor fool's neck and drank until the vampire began to crumble into dust. Hunger sated for the moment, Richard went back to worrying about Kieran Belle's safety.

CHAPTER THIRTEEN

Kieran stood on the beach holding his camera, watching Cory and Billy playing fetch along the edge of the surf. Cory was only wearing surfer style board shorts as he tossed a stick for Billy to chase. Kieran regarded the two playing and rough housing as Billy tired of chasing the stick, pounced on Cory, and knocked him on his butt in the sand. He raised his camera and began snapping pictures. Cory was his favorite model to photograph. Cory possessed a quality the camera loved, or perhaps the quality was the fact the photographer was in love with the subject the camera caught. When the camera stopped advancing the film, Kieran put the camera away and went to join Cory and Billy.

Cory noted Kieran's approach down the beach and marveled at the play of Kieran's muscles beneath his skin. Kieran's swim trunks were a square cut boxer style and outlined his bulge and ass to perfection. Since their first night on the beach, Kieran had left his hair loose or tied back with a single leather thong at the base of his neck. As Kieran jogged down the beach toward where Billy and he were playing, Cory noted his lover had left his hair unbound and the waist-length mane fluttered out behind him. Billy spotted Kieran and raced down the beach toward him. The wolf leapt and collided with Kieran, driving the wind from the young man's lungs, and knocked him to the ground. The two rolled down the beach, getting covered in sand. Watching the pair, Cory thought about the small box buried in a side pocket of his pack. He'd carefully kept it hidden from Kieran since they left the Cooper family farm. All he needed was the courage to ask a simple question. Cory laughed at the pair and jogged over to help his lover back to his feet. Both Billy and Kieran shook themselves off, sending sand everywhere and making Cory cover his face as the sand flew his way.

"Hey, you two, stop."

Kieran laughed at the expression on Cory's face before grabbing his hand and dragging him into the surf. The lovers swam for a while before heading back up the beach to their campsite to dry off and prepare lunch. When they'd finished eating, Cory reached out and ran his fingers through Kieran's hair as he pulled him close for a kiss. His fingers caught in the salt-matted hair, and Kieran winced in pain at the tug.

"Sorry, babe. I didn't mean to pull your hair."

"Everything's okay, Wolf. The hazard of hair this long around the ocean, I'm not even sure why I ever grew my hair this long other than to spite Grandmother's sense of what's proper for men."

"Well, I love the length and the silky texture of your hair under normal conditions, but we're going to need to get the salt out before your hair is a total wreck."

"Let's grab our kits, towels, and some clothes. I've got a place I want to show you and we can soak in something besides salt water."

"What is this place?"

"A surprise I think you'll enjoy."

The young men grabbed their shower kits, towels, and changes of clothes and threw on their socks and boots. They tossed the gear into daypacks before heading out. The path Kieran set them on climbed the cliffs further down the beach from where they'd come down to the shore from their cabin. After about an hour of hiking, they arrived at the opening to a cave high above the ocean surf. Kieran lead the way inside, and when the way twisted around a corner and the sun was blocked, he stopped for a moment to let Cory's and his eyes adjust to the darkness and the faint traces of bioluminescence. Cory's indrawn breath of surprise after his eyes adjusted confirmed to Kieran choosing to show him this place was the right thing to do. Kieran took Cory's hand and led the way deeper into the cave system. Cory made out the sound of running water in the distance. Soon, a different source of light brightened the cave and reflected off a pool of water. The light came from veins of quartz in the walls stretched to the surface. Cory's gaze penetrated the dark to recognize where places for torches were set around the walls of the cave.

"This is beautiful, Kieran."

"If you will tolerate my magic for a moment, Cory, I can truly bring the beauty here to life for you."

"For you, I'll endure anything."

Kieran kissed his lover, turned, and made a strange gesture with his hands before slapping his left hand against the wall. Silver magic spread from his fingers to form a spider web of illumination as the magic flowed around the cavern. In the places where his magic touched the crystals set into the walls, they burst into silver light, brightening the cavern to early afternoon illumination. Before Cory, stretched a series of natural pools and a small waterfall, the source of the running water sound he'd made out as they made their way here. A couple of the pools appeared to be steaming hot springs.

"This can't all be natural."

"No, everything is shaped by magic, mostly Emerald, Sapphire, and Ruby. The lighting system is shaped with Silver magic, which also acts as a ward against intruders when activated."

"This place is amazing, but I thought your family only possessed Silver magic."

"The men of the family only possess Silver magic. Like your father, Grams practices Sapphire magic. My late great-aunt had Ruby magic and her husband had Emerald; they're the ones who shaped this place along with Gramps."

"Well, this place is beautiful."

"We can put our things over here."

Kieran lead the way over to a stone bench in a nook designed with hooks for towels and clothes around the walls. The young men stripped off their boots, socks, and shorts. Naked, they followed a smooth path down to the level of the pools. They made their way over to the pool at the base of the waterfall and eased themselves in. The water came to their waists as the walked across to the waterfall. To Cory's amazement, the water temperature hovered around body temperature instead of being ice cold. He followed Kieran under the waterfall and helped him rinse as much of the salt out of his hair. They realized they left their kits back on the bench. Kieran lead Cory back toward where they left their things and settled him into a warm pool with carved benches around the rim about a foot below the surface. Kieran walked back to their things and grabbed their kit bags. Cory admired the beauty of his naked lover's muscles flexing beneath his skin as he walked away to get their kits. The play of Kieran's waist-length hair across the top of his firm bubble butt made Cory's cock firm up fast. Watching Kieran's soft, thick cock swaying over his plump ball sack gave Cory a hard-on. As Kieran stepped down into the pool near where Cory sat, Cory moved enough to take Kieran's soft cock into his mouth and began to tease the head with his tongue. Kieran moaned as Cory's tongue bathed his cock and brought the shaft to its full length and hardness. Cory buried his nose in Kieran's well-trimmed pubic hair and inhaled the scent of his lover as he worked over the hard shaft with his tongue, lips, throat, and using his teeth to tease.

Kieran buried his hands in Cory's thick blond hair as he giggled as his lover's beard tickled his balls on each downward motion of Cory's head. He remembered complimenting the bearded appearance when Cory first started to grow one. He complained about the beard the first time they made out when Cory started letting the beard grow, when the beard scratched in those early stages of growth. Now Cory's thick, soft beard added an extra layer of pleasure to their lovemaking when Cory applied his oral skills to either Kieran's cock or ass. With a deep moan of pleasure, Kieran filled his lover's mouth with his seed. He stepped back enough to free his sensitive cock from Cory's ministrations. Cory loved to work Kieran's cock beyond his orgasm to keep him hard and to try to coax a quick, second load from Kieran's still tingling balls. If Kieran didn't leave room or leverage to withdraw, Cory would win the mini battle and enjoy the cries of pleasure-filled anguish coming from deep in Kieran's chest.

This time Kieran had room to escape, though he didn't go far. Once his cock was clear of Cory's mouth, Kieran dropped to his knees in the pool between Cory's legs, and leaning forward, captured his lover's throbbing cock in his mouth to return the favor. Kieran enjoyed the sensation of Cory wrapping his fingers into his hair, one of his favorite things to do to softly guide Kieran's pace. Cory's moans of pleasure increased when Kieran relaxed his gag reflex and let his lover's thick cock slip deep into his throat. Before long, Cory was on the edge, and his tightening grip dragged Kieran down to the root of his cock, driving the head into the younger man's throat as he blew his thick load. After the first blast rocketed down his throat, Kieran was able to slide back up Cory's shaft and take the rest of his lover's load into his mouth. Despite the number of times he'd swallowed, Cory's load was still a strange burning sensation and bitter flavor in his mouth. He didn't care this was a part of Cory, and for a while, it would be a part of him. When Cory's orgasm ended, Kieran licked his lover clean before pulling off and dragging Cory into the pool.

The lovers went under the surface and emerged locked in each other's arms in a deep kiss. Kieran's hair formed a soggy curtain around both of their faces and kept them from noticing a shadow move across the cavern and into a hidden alcove. With reluctance, they separated from each other before they waded back to the edge of the pool, and Cory grabbed the shampoo from the ledge before Kieran reached the bottle. He turned Kieran so his back was to him and squirted a decent amount of shampoo into his hand before proceeding to lather up Kieran's hair. Having his scalp massaged always put Kieran into a trance-like state of pleasure. Cory loved listening to Kieran's faint moans as he worked his fingers over his head and down his neck. He was never sure how Kieran managed to keep his hair clean on his own but suspected magic played a role in the process somehow. Once Kieran discovered how much Cory loved to play with his hair, he'd become shameless in allowing Cory to wash his hair for him at least twice a week. Cory used his handhold on Kieran's hair to bend his lover's head back and steal a kiss before dunking him to rinse the shampoo out of the midnight locks. Once they washed away all traces of salt and sand, Kieran led them over to another pool of warm clean water. It was big enough for two people to share while lying down. The lovers entwined on the low shelf, which put most of their bodies underwater as they began to tease and caress each other. They brought each other to climax and viewed their seed flowing and mixing in the water before drifting off to the pool's drainage system. Kieran and Cory pulled themselves from the pool and padded over to where they'd left their towels and clothes to dry off before Kieran picked up his kit and led Cory naked into a smaller side chamber designed for sleeping or making love, he never quite decided what his grandparents, great-aunt, and great-uncle had crafted this chamber for. Here, he dug out lube and condoms, and set them on the small shelf beside the large padded outcropping, which served as a bed. Now in this smaller chamber, Kieran's dominate personality slipped away as he let Cory take the lead in their lovemaking. Cory bent Kieran over the edge of the outcropping forming the base of the bed. He spread Kieran's ass cheeks, and kneeling behind his lover, began to lick and rim the exposed hole. Kieran gave himself over to Cory's ministrations. Pleasure soon overwhelmed any thought process in Kieran's mind as Cory relaxed the muscles of his hole and began to slide a finger in to begin loosening him for entry. Kieran wanted to reach down and take himself in hand but remembered from previous experience if he did, Cory would stop and replace tongue and fingers with the flat of his hand in a spanking. During one of their nights of passion back in

Little Rock, Cory had stopped rimming him, flipped him face down, made Kieran count the spanks, and thank him for them afterward. Their agreement stated, unless otherwise arranged, Cory was the boss in the bedroom.

Cory reached up with his other hand and pulled Kieran's cock and balls back between his legs to tease them with his tongue as he worked on his lover's ass. The tongue traced upward from the tip of Kieran's cock, along the shaft, over the tightening ball sack, and along the taint into the crack before circling the edge of the hole. Tongue plunged deep into the hole elicited deep moans of pleasure from its owner and a copious amount of pre-cum to leak from the tip of the cock. Kieran shivered as his lover teased him again and again to the brink of coming, only to back off and deny release. Before long, he found himself begging Cory to fuck him. Taking mercy on his prostrate lover, Cory rose and grabbed a condom from nearby. He suited up, added enough lube to make entry painless, and slid his cock into Kieran's ass to the hilt on the first push.

"Oh, Bright Goddess, yes! Oh, how I've needed you to do this to me, Wolf. Take my ass and make me yours," Kieran wailed in pleasure.

"You crave these times I take full control like this, don't you, lover? You need to let go of everything and be. To be owned by someone who will never let you go."

"Yes, yes. Take me, own me, and never let me go. I need you more than you will ever realize, Wolf."

Cory slid in and out of Kieran's ass until his lover shuddered beneath him, and with a silent sob of joy, exploded in a full body orgasm. Kieran's cock still pinned back between his legs exploded as his whole body achieved orgasm and splattered the back of his legs and Cory's feet to the ankles. Cory pulled out and removed the full condom, making sure not to let the contents spill, as Kieran collapsed on the bed and slid to his knees. Once the condom was disposed of, Cory returned to his lover and helped him stand. They made their way back down to the bathing pools where Cory cleaned them both up. Kieran revived as Cory ran the washcloth over his still sensitive cock head. He grabbed his lover's hand and stopped the torment. He wrestled the cloth away from Cory, and with lots of love, washed his body from head to toe, taking extra care around Cory's cock and balls. When they were cleaned up, they went back to the bedchamber and cleaned the room up before turning in for the night. Cory settled in first, and Kieran climbed in beside him, settling in with his head resting on Cory's furry chest. Cory's steady breathing soon had Kieran drifting away on the edges of sleep. Strong fingers stroked through Kieran's hair; finding the places on his scalp relaxed him and sent him to sleep.

Cory lay watching his lover drift off into peaceful sleep.

CHAPTER FOURTEEN

Kieran and Cory spent the last day of their escape swimming and playing along the ocean shore. They packed away all their gear and stowed the equipment away in the cavern before cooking dinner together.

"I think you're extra special. You have a second magic about you when you're in the kitchen."

"I spent a lot of time in the kitchen both here and at home with Mom's family. Cooking at the Belle estate kept me out of the way of Grandmother and the rest of the Matriarchs. Here, Grams loves to cook and she loves to teach. When we get back to Little Rock, I'm going to spoil you with a proper home-cooked meal."

"I need to increase my exercise regiment if I let you do the cooking."

"We're both going to have to up our exercise routines, Wolf. I want you to start training with me so you can pick up some decent self-defense skills."

"Kieran, I've never been a fighter. I'll train with you, but I'm never going to be anywhere near your level."

"I'm not worried about you matching my skill level, Wolf. What I want is for you to be able to hold off an attacker long enough either for me to get to you or for you to find a way to escape."

"As long as we agree you aren't training me to enter any *Fight Club* events."

"I promise this will be a strict bully deterring 101."

Wrapping his arms around Kieran's lean waist, Cory pulled his lover back against him and nuzzled his nose into Kieran's neck in the wolfish way, which drove his lover nuts. Cory turned his lover's head and kissed him before letting him go to finish cooking. Kieran sighed and refocused on their dinner. After dinner, they retired to the sleeping chamber, and they made love.

****

In the morning, they packed up their clothes and personal gear, and headed back to the main residences of the compound. At the top of the path leading back to their cabin, Cory stopped to gaze out over the ocean one more time. Kieran came up beside him and wrapped an arm around Cory's waist.

"When we finish the rituals, which will grant me proper access to the powers of the Silver Witch, we'll come back here, Wolf. In the family grimoire is a ritual, which will let us complete our mating bond without worrying about what the magic in our blood might do to each of us. This is a full moon ritual, so we'll have to wait until next month before we try the ritual."

"So we can be mated, I can wait another month for whatever we need to do."

"Well, I found this one ritual we might do with a quick trip into town, Wolf."

"What ritual do you mean, Kieran?"

Kieran dropped his pack, sank down on one knee, and presented Cory with a small box. Cory glanced at Kieran, stared at the box, and back at Kieran again. His heart fluttered. Was Kieran thinking the same thing he'd been thinking all week? Kieran smiled and opened the box to reveal a gold ring set with a moonstone and a matching set of gold rings etched with the Gaelic phrase, *Deo mo chroí*, forever my heart.

"Corwin Samuel Cooper, will you do me the honor of becoming my husband?" Kieran said as he took the moonstone ring from the box and placed the ring at the tip of Cory's left ring finger, since the soul mate band, which had once occupied the finger, was gone.

Cory eyes, actually brimming with tears, gazed down into Kieran's silver eyes. He smiled and answered with one word. "Yes."

Kieran slipped the ring on Cory's finger and kissed his lover's hand. Before he rose to take Cory in his arms, his lover's pack was on the ground beside his own, and Cory was now gazing into his eyes from the same level. Amber eyes burned with love and devotion as Cory raised a similar small box up into Kieran's line of sight.

"I guess I'm silly to ask you the same question in return," Cory said as he opened his box to reveal a gold ring set with an uncut canary-yellow diamond and placing the ring at the tip of Kieran's left ring finger. "But, Kieran Samuel Belle Oisín, will you do me the honor of becoming my husband?"

Silver eyes locked with amber eyes across the tiny distance, and Cory realized he needed no vocal response as he witnessed the love burn for him in Kieran's eyes. Kieran struggled to speak around the lump, which was wedged deep in his throat, so he nodded his head in the affirmative. Cory slipped the ring on Kieran's finger, and he too kissed his lover's hand. Reaching out, Kieran drew Cory into a deep kiss, which only broke when the lovers ran out of air in their lungs.

They stared at each other and laughed.

"I can't believe we both came up with the same idea," Kieran said between giggles.

"This is a crazy situation, although I didn't pick out matching wedding bands. I thought we would pick them out together."

"Actually, I didn't pick them out. I inherited them from my mother. She left me hers in her will, much to Grandmother's annoyance. Dad put his in the box on the day they read mother's will, and he understood her wish. She also left me the engagement ring, which is an heirloom as well."

"Well, the ring I gave you isn't an heirloom, but I did find the diamond myself down at the Crater of Diamonds State Park, back home in Arkansas. I mounted the stone uncut so the person I gave the ring to would understand my love is as raw as the diamond on his finger."

"Such a beautiful ring, Wolf, and the diamond will always remind me of your eyes."

"So what does the writing say on the wedding bands?"

"*Deo mo chroí*, which means 'forever my heart.' The man Beauty chose to be her eldest daughter's husband gave her these bands when they married in his native Ireland. Rumor says the prince gave this engagement ring to Beauty. I don't how much is true and how much is legend. All I care about is my parents used these wedding bands last, and Mother broke tradition by giving them to me. They should have gone to my eldest sister."

"It's an honor to be married using your parents' rings. I don't care who else legend says wore them. So, I'm guessing the ritual in town is to go before the clerk of the court and do the paperwork and say our vows."

"Yes, we'll go to the town offices, do the paperwork, and appear before a notary to get our marriage recognized. You realize, of course, we'll need to have witnesses, because Grams, for one, will never forgive me if I elope."

"Oh no, we are not getting your grams upset with us. I don't care what the rest of your family thinks of me. I'm not upsetting Grams. Come on, let's get back so we can surprise your family at dinner tonight."

****

After returning to their cabin, the young lovers got cleaned up and put on dressy clothes before heading over to the main house for dinner with the rest of Kieran's family. While Kieran's grandmother finished getting the food ready, the boys joined Kieran's grandfather, father, and uncle in the family room. None of the older men paid attention to the near idiotic grins of joy on either of the young men's faces. Grams entered the family room to announce dinner and stopped short when she spotted the excited expressions on Kieran's and Cory's faces being ignored by her husband and sons.

"Honestly, I'm amazed at how dense the men of this family can be. I've told you that all your attempts to hurt or separate the boys are over. They've both passed all of your tests, so get over your plotting. I'll not have Cory thinking this family is anything like the House of Beauty. Shame on you, Kellen Kieran Oisín, for failing to recognize your own son and his boyfriend have news."

Kellen and Brom turned to face the boys and espied Cory standing in a possessive position behind Kieran, their left hands clasped over their right hands. Brom spotted the Belle engagement ring on Cory's left ring finger first. He also spotted the unusual ring on Kieran's hand on the same finger.

"So which of you asked the other one first?" Brom asked.

"What are you talking about, Brom?" Kellen asked.

"For the super witch of the family, you are so dense, little brother."

"What am I missing?"

Kieran raised his and Cory's left hands and held them out to his father so the rings appeared under his nose, and the boys said in unison, "He asked me to marry him, and I said yes."

Kellen dragged both boys into a fierce hug, which quickly turned into a family hug as Brom, Grams, and Gramps joined in to congratulate the boys. All the tension of the past few weeks seemed to melt away over the joyous news. When the hug finally broke, Grams urged everyone into the dining room so they might eat while they discussed the plans for Kieran and Cory's handfasting. Cory appeared confused by the terms Grams and Gramps tossed around. Kieran took pity on his fiancé and leaned close to explain after stealing a quick kiss.

"A handfasting is the old religion's version of marriage, only more than the church or the state's version of marriage, Wolf. Both parties declare their intention and they're marrying of their own free will, not reciting forced vows."

"Oh, I like the sound of this. So I guess this means no one in your family was ever forced into a shotgun handfasting."

"No, Wolf. You can't force anyone into a handfasting; the goddess and the god would never bless a forced union. The choice is up to you if you want to go through the ceremony. If you don't want to because of a conflict with your own beliefs, I'll understand, and we won't be any less married because we didn't get handfasted."

"I've never been much of a church goer. I've only ever gone because Mom and Dad were big on us doing everything as a family. I'm about to become a member of your family, or we're starting our own family, so we should have our own traditions, and if they're a blend of both, I don't think the divine will be too upset with us."

"You'll find our traditions are pretty blended in this family. I don't think we're going to get much say in how the ceremony is done, only whether we want to participate. As I said, they can't force us to be handfasted. They didn't even insist on offering ceremony to Mom and Dad when they announced their engagement."

"What about your mother's family? Will they attend?"

Kieran snorted in indignation. "No, Grandmother Belle would never lower herself to attend a ritual of the old religion. She's High Church."

Cory was sad; part of Kieran's family wouldn't be in attendance, but the expression on Kieran's face said he was glad they wouldn't be around to disrupt the ceremony. A cough from Grams' end of the table dragged both boys' attention to the Matriarch of the Oisín clan.

"I'm asking, dear boy, if you and Cory both agree to be handfasted. Do try to pay attention."

"Sorry, Grams, I was trying to explain to Cory what everyone else was talking about before you got him to agree to something he doesn't want."

"Of course, so now he understands what we're talking about, what's your decision?"

"We agree to be handfasted, Grams. Will you and Gramps consent to be High Priestess and High Priest for our handfasting?"

87

"Of course, we would be honored to serve in those roles, Kieran. We will need to invite a few other mages to properly call the quarters. Do you have anyone you want to attend the ceremony?"

"If the ceremony doesn't offend them, I think we need to invite Cory's parents, and if we blend traditions enough, Cory's dad might agree to serve as the Western Guardian, since he's a Sapphire mage. What do you think, Wolf?"

"I think they'll come because they'll be mad if we don't at least invite them."

"I want to invite Professor Mason, which will give us an Emerald mage for the Northern Guardian. I don't recall any Ruby mages I can call or...wait, I can ask one if he'll come. Mr. St. Martin would be perfect for the Southern Guardian since he's a hunter as well as having Ruby magic."

"Good, Kieran, after dinner, let's call Cory's parents and invite them, and if you'll let me speak to Cory's father, Sapphire mage to Sapphire mage, I think I can convince him to serve."

"Oops, I almost forgot to ask, Wolf. We need to take precautions to protect the barrier spell. Can your mother control the shift? This is a full moon ritual, and if she shifts, the ceremony won't be ruined, but the shift will cause other problems."

"Yes, she's only ever shifted when she's wanted or needed to do so."

"Okay, filling the Eastern Guardian's position is the only thing left. Dad, I gather from reading the ceremony in the family's grimoire, by tradition, the heir to the Silver Witch stands as the Eastern Guardian, but I need you at full strength for the other ritual Cory and I want to undergo during the full moon, so would you mind if Uncle Brom stood in the East for our handfasting?"

"Since I think I can guess the other ritual you're talking about, Kieran, I don't mind letting Brom take my place in the East. I think perhaps your grandfather and I should switch roles and let me be the High Priest for your handfasting while he serves as guardian for your second ritual."

"What is this second ritual, Kieran?" Gramps asked.

"The mate-binding ritual. Cory and I need and want to mate at least once without barriers so his mating drive is locked into me and I'm locked into him. We can't make love to mate if I retain my magic, because we wouldn't be able to tell what would happen if our opposing magic touched when our body fluids meet inside either of us. Only you or Dad are powerful enough to draw out my magic during the night of the full moon."

"You're choosing a perilous ritual, Grandson. Not only for the two of you, but for the guardian of the ritual. If anything happened to me during the ritual, you might never get your magic back."

"I understand, Gramps. This is why I asked Dad to stand as guardian. Health wise, he's younger and stronger than you are. Magic wise, he's between us in power, and as your direct heir, he is able to call on your power to help him if something goes wrong. I'll leave the decision up to you two to discuss and decide."

The discussion ended as everyone began to dig into dinner. After dinner, Cory and Grams retired to the kitchen to call his parents while Kieran went with his father and Gramps to the library to discuss the mate-binding ritual in further details. Brom left to return to his own cabin near his forge.

INTERLUDE: THE BARRIER DISCOVERED

Alex Kincaid and the small group of shifters they gave him searched for weeks along the back roads of coastal Maine for a trace of Kieran Belle and Cory Cooper. The special compass he possessed didn't work to specifications. The needle kept spinning madly around, never settling in to point out where his quarry lay. At the directions of the mysterious Master, several additional shifters arrived from the dark Alpha's pack to help him locate his prey. He didn't trust any of the shifters to guard his back beyond this mission, and one of them he didn't trust at all. The girl, Marissa Holden, didn't seem ruthless enough to be a member of the dark Alpha's pack and survive.

The little female shifter came wrapped in Ebony magic. Control spells wrapped around Marissa so tight she only followed certain outside orders. Kincaid didn't understand why the mysterious Master sent this particular shifter since she, unlike the others he'd been sent, needed so many controls.

At the next turning on yet another dusty dirt road, Kincaid learned why the girl was sent.

"Stop here. Kieran passed by here."

"How can you tell?"

"By his scent and his power. Let me out so I can find his path."

Kincaid stopped the van and let the Marissa and two other shifters out to locate the path. Sniffing the air, the girl moved around and came to a stop about two hundred feet to the right of the van. She pointed. "His trail goes this way."

Kincaid stared at where she pointed and surveyed only trees. He gestured to one of the shifters, and the man raced ahead. About a hundred feet past the girl, he slammed into a barrier of some sort, screamed, and burst into flames.

"What the hell?" Kincaid screamed at the girl.

"Defense spell. Only the invited may cross."

"Why didn't you say something?"

"You didn't ask or order me to give you a warning."

After a brief moment of confusion, Kincaid's fiery temper burst. He lost control and smashed his fist into her solar plexus, driving the wind from her lungs and sending her to the ground where he beat her until she lost consciousness. He ordered his remaining shifters to check how far the barrier ran. *This is going to take longer than planned.* Time to come up with a plan B, in case he needed one.

CHAPTER FIFTEEN

A couple of days after getting engaged and setting the date for his handfasting to Cory, Kieran checked his cell phone for the first time in a couple of weeks and discovered the message from Richard St. Martin. He listened to the warning the hunter left him, and his blood grew cold, causing a shiver to run up his back. He quickly found Richard's number and returned his call.

"St. Martin's Antiques and Collectibles. How can we help you today?" came Richard's voice over the phone.

"Mr. St. Martin, this is Kieran Belle."

"Kieran, I've been worried sick. When I didn't get a call back from you right away, I feared the worst, but when I couldn't find you by magical means, I realized Kincaid wouldn't be able to do so either."

"Yes, a locator spell to find me would take a powerful Ebony mage to cast to pierce the spells I'm under. Thank you for the warning, Mr. St. Martin. I'll keep an eye peeled for any signs of him."

"Good, I realize you'll be careful. You possess the instincts to make a spectacular hunter, even if you are a male of the House of Beauty."

"I'm glad you think so, because I'm the current hunter-candidate of the House of Beauty. All my sisters failed the test."

"I'm sorry to learn your sisters failed Kieran, and I'm sorry for your loss. I trust you will lead the House of Beauty into a new era."

"Thank you, Richard. I need to ask a favor of you if you can travel and don't mind participating in a Pagan ritual. I would like you to stand as Southern Guardian at my handfasting to Cory on the 31st of July."

"I'm honored to be asked, Kieran, but I'm sorry, I made a promise to my fiancée before her death to give up my Pagan ways, and even though she's gone, I intend to keep my promise in honor of her memory."

"I'm sorry, I didn't even consider the idea you might be engaged. Of course I wouldn't want you to break a promise, and I understand."

"Well, you be sure to bring your husband by so I can meet him when you're out this way."

"I will, Richard. Thank you."

"You're welcome, Kieran, and congratulations."

The phone clicked off from Richard's end, and Kieran turned his phone off again. They would need to be careful when they went into Bar Harbor to get the marriage license and appeared before the notary to make their marriage legal under Maine law.

CHAPTER SIXTEEN

Later in the afternoon, following his call to Richard St. Martin; Kieran and Cory sat on the couch with Kieran between Cory's legs and leaning back against his lover's chest as they filled out Maine's Intention of Marriage form on a laptop perched on Kieran's knees. As they filled out the forms, Cory made mental note of Kieran's fast approaching birthday, knowing he'd need to arrange something with Grams and the rest of the family. They wanted to have everything ready for a trip into Bar Harbor to file for their marriage license and certificate. They were double-checking their information on the form before printing the form out when Uncle Brom knocked on the door to their cabin.

"Come on in, Uncle Brom. The door is open," Kieran called.

"Hey, guys, I realize you have rings and everything for your handfasting, but I wanted to do something for you," Brom said.

"You're doing enough by being the Eastern Guardian, Uncle Brom. You don't have to do anything else," Kieran told his uncle.

"Well, I thought you guys should have an honeymoon after we get all the paperwork done and filed. I figured you'd have to go before a judge or notary in town for an official marriage since neither Mom nor Dad is a licensed member of a clergy. Therefore, I booked you three nights at the Black Friar Inn. The inn is only a block away from the town offices and walking distance to all the attractions of Bar Harbor."

"Uncle Brom, this is a wonderful gift. What do you think, Wolf? Want to play honeymooning tourists with me?" Kieran teased Cory.

"I can think of several things I'd like to play with you, future Mr. Cooper."

"Oh you think so, future Mr. Oisín, or would you rather be the future Mr. Belle?"

"Okay, boys, I'm going to escape before I get drawn into this one," Brom said, raising his hands as he backed away from the boys. "Oh yeah, one last question. Which one of you gets the bachelor party and which one gets the bridal shower?"

Brom ducked and dodged the pillows, which were hurled his way as he stepped out of the cabin.

"So, in all seriousness, do we pick one family name or the other, or do we choose to hyphenate our names in some fashion?"

"I guess we're going to have to hyphenate names. I'm not sure I want to be Kieran Samuel Belle-Cooper-Oisín though, too much of a mouthful."

"Yeah, all those names are a bit much. I guess the question is which family will be the most disappointed in not being in our family name."

"Well, I don't have a problem with dropping the Belle part of my name, even though I'm likely to be the hunter for the House of Beauty by the end of the summer. I'd be happy being Kieran Samuel Oisín-Cooper or even plain Kieran Cooper," Kieran said with a grin.

"Well, as much as I'd like to have you take my name, I don't think we should drop your father's family name from our new family, so I can be happy with Oisín-Cooper as well," Cory said before kissing the top of Kieran's head.

Kieran set the laptop down on the coffee table and turned so his cheek was pressed against Cory's chest, and his lover wrapped him tighter in his arms.

"I like the sound of Mr. and Mr. Oisín-Cooper, Wolf, although the name change is going to create a nightmare of paperwork back at school."

"I like the sound of the new name too. We'll deal with the paperwork when we get back to school, if we're going back to school. Won't you have to stay here if you're the next hunter?"

"No, I can move the family seat wherever I choose to claim as my territory. We can even put the scare into your brother Jeff and his pack by claiming your parents' farm as the new seat of the House of Beauty."

"Oh my, you would rock his Alpha ass back a few steps. I think we should find someplace we can call our own, especially if we're going to raise a family to keep the House of Beauty going."

"Let's not worry about the future of the House of Beauty for now, Wolf. Let's enjoy some normal time together before we start worrying too much about the future."

Kieran snuggled in tighter to his lover, and Cory stroked Kieran's hair and enjoyed the warmth of his lover's body against his own. The two of them drifted off to sleep on the couch, content and safe in the other's arms.

When they woke later in the afternoon, they kissed and stretched to get the kinks out from their somewhat awkward sleeping arrangement. Kieran scooped up his phone from the coffee table.

"I should call Professor Mason and ask him if he will participate in our handfasting."

"Go ahead, Kieran. I'll go fix us a light snack while you talk to the professor." Cory kissed Kieran on the forehead as he got off the couch and headed to the kitchen.

Dialing his professor's number, Kieran waited as the phone rang several times before Professor Mason answered. "John Mason Photography. How can I help you?" The professor's deep baritone voice rumbled through the phone.

"Professor Mason, hi, this is Kieran Belle."

"Kieran, I thought you and Cory were in Maine for the summer. Are you guys okay?"

"We're fine, professor. Actually, we're getting married in a couple of days. We wondered if you might be available to come to Maine for a few days to participate in our handfasting ceremony on July 31?"

"Congratulations, Kieran, and please give my congratulations to Cory as well. I think I can get away around your date for a few days. What do you need from me by way of participation? I'm pretty rusty on the handfasting front."

"We would like you to stand as the Northern Guardian. We would also love for you to do our wedding photographs after the ceremony."

"Let me check into flights and make sure I'm not committed to anything else, and I'll call you back in a day or so to give you an update, Kieran."

"Thank you, Professor." Kieran hung up as Cory returned with a plate of cheese and summer sausage and two bottled waters.

"From the grin on your face, I gather Professor Mason said yes," Cory said as he set down the plate and handed Kieran a bottle of water.

"Well, he didn't say no. He has to check to make sure he doesn't have other plans and can get away around the date. He's going to check flights and call back. He sends his congratulations," Kieran replied as he cracked open the water bottle.

"I'm glad you asked him. Mom and Dad are coming, and Dad was excited about having a part in the ceremony. Mom said Dad is enchanting a special necklace for her, which will keep her shift at bay until she takes the pendant off."

"Glad we checked in on their plans. I don't want to cause your mother pain, but shifting once she's inside the barrier spell would be a bad thing. A shift would bring the barrier down and leave the whole compound vulnerable to attack."

"Babe, what a terrifying thought. No wonder your grandfather was so anxious when he learned Billy was a shifter. If anything happens to the collar while we're here—"

"Everything is okay, Wolf. The collar isn't coming off unless Billy agrees to have the collar removed or an Ebony mage equal to me in power breaks the spell."

The young men dug into their snack and relaxed on the couch until the food was gone. When they were finished, Kieran took the plate and the empty bottles back to the kitchen to clean up before they headed out to visit Uncle Brom at his forge.

INTERLUDE: THE RENEGADE HUNTER'S PLAN B

Alex Kincaid left a pair of his shifters behind to keep an eye on the barrier spell and the supposed path into the area where his target was hiding. He took the rest of his forces and headed into Bar Harbor to set up a base of operations since the town was the closest one. Kincaid figured the target or someone supporting him would have to leave and get supplies at some point. The watchers would alert Kincaid, and he would set a trap for the boy or whoever came to town. If he captured the boy, he might finally get paid; if they captured someone else, he'd have leverage to get the boy where he wanted him. He set his shifters up in various parts of the town, or village as the place called itself, and got himself a room at the Harborside Hotel. Once he settled in, he contacted Professor Simms to update him on the changes to the plan. To say the man wasn't happy was an understatement, but Kincaid informed him of everything. Unless a powerful Ebony mage was handy, they wouldn't get past the barrier spell. Now a waiting game began.

CHAPTER SEVENTEEN

On Friday, the Oisín family along with Kieran and Cory piled into the family's large passenger van for the trip to Bar Harbor. The excited young men put their weekend bag in the back of the van before taking the bench seat at the rear of the van. Uncle Brom got behind the wheel to drive with Kellen in the front passenger seat. Kieran's grandparents took the middle row of seats. When everyone was buckled in, Brom started the van and headed for the gates of the estate. As the van passed through the gates of the estate and out on the road, which would take them out to Highway 3, none of the passengers spotted the watchers who noted several people leaving the hideaway. The family chatted away during the drive to Bar Harbor and recommended activities for the young couple in the back to think about doing during their short honeymoon.

"Make sure you take Cory out on the whale sighting and lighthouse tour, Kieran. You always loved going when you were a boy," Grams said.

"I promise I will make sure Cory gets the full Bar Harbor experience. I hope everything goes right in town today. Grams, did you manage to contact your friend about standing as the Southern Guardian?"

"Yes, dear. Emma. You remember Mrs. Handler, don't you, dear? You had her in school the year you and your father stayed with us."

"She was my fifth grade teacher, Grams. Does Mrs. Handler still remember me?" Kieran appeared a little worried.

"Okay, what did you do to this woman when she was your teacher?" Cory asked, knowing if Kieran didn't give him the answer, Grams would.

"Oh lord, this is embarrassing. Grams and Gramps sent me to the private school where Mrs. Handler taught gifted students how to control their magic. I was a horrible showoff because I'd been learning to use my magic for a couple of years. I also had the horrible problem of wanting to be the center of attention. So, Mrs. Handler decided one day I needed a special lesson." Kieran turned bright red in embarrassment and couldn't continue.

"So what happened?" Cory grinned, enjoying watching his fiancé blush and squirm.

"Dear Emma decided—since Kieran liked to showoff and acted like a bully—to let all the other kids get in a magical whack at him. She slipped a special training potion into Kieran's drink at lunchtime, which blocked his magic for the afternoon. When he started to bully one of the other boys and went to back his threat up with magic, he found himself defenseless. That's when the boy got mad and lashed out at him with a fireball. When the other kids he bullied realized he couldn't defend himself with magic, Kieran learned firsthand what he put them all through. Mrs. Handler made Kieran apologize to each student he bullied. The experience humbled our poor Kieran the way he needed."

"She was right to do what she did. I was so in the wrong, and I moped for hours afterward. When she figured I'd learned my lesson, she had all the other kids apologize to me for doing back to me what I'd done to them. I'm still not sure some of them forgave me. Afterward, I went out of my way to stop other powerful kids from bullying those with less power."

"Well, the lesson stuck with you. I've seen you face bullies on campus, plus the time you rescued Billy when Johnson got mad at him."

"Yeah, bullying isn't right. One of my classmates in high school was ready to commit suicide because the head cheerleader and her crew were bullying her. I caught her before she took the pills. To prove to her how easily bullying can be overcome, I recruited the help of a few friends at school, and we got her elected Junior Prom Queen and the president of the chess club elected as her Prom King. The expressions on the faces of the so-called in-crowd were priceless. Last, information I received, they were planning their wedding."

"Yes, they got married before you boys left Arkansas to come up here," Grams said.

"Hey, we'll be in town in a few minutes, so make sure you have everything," Brom called out.

Kieran and Cory reached for each other's hand and laughed as they both realized how nervous the other one was. They turned to gaze at each other, and their eyes spoke volumes about how much they loved each other. The van made the turn from the highway to Cottage Street and pulled into the parking lot for the city office building. Once the van was parked, they all climbed out and made their way into the office building to find the correct office for filing the Intention of Marriage form and pay the fees to get their marriage license and certificate. Only one other couple was in line ahead of them, so the wait to file and get the forms was only about the forty minutes the website mentioned the process would take to get the license, the certificate would be sent to them after the license was signed and turned in by the official who performed the service. Kieran asked if a notary was on duty to perform the brief civil service and deal with the paperwork, and they were directed to an office downstairs. After exchanging brief vows and signing the license before witnesses and the notary, Kieran and Cory were pronounced married by the laws of the State of Maine. For once, Cory moved faster than Kieran. He grabbed him and kissed him when the notary said they were now legal spouses.

"I love you, Mr. Oisín-Cooper," Cory said when he broke the kiss.

"And, I love you too, Mr. Oisín-Cooper," came Kieran's breathless response.

"Congratulations, gentlemen," the notary said as he handed them their copy of the license. "I'll get this filed, and you should receive your marriage certificate in about thirty days."

"Thank you," Kieran replied as he took the form, and with care, put the license away in the file folder, which held all the original paperwork before handing the folder over to his father.

The newlyweds and family exited the town office building and piled back into the van to head around the block to Summer Street where the Black Friar Inn was located. Uncle Brom informed them he'd reserved the room under Cory's name, guessing they might take at least Cory's family name. The young men laughed as they slid from the van and gathered their bags from the back of the van. They headed inside to the check-in desk, and the clerk found their reservation.

"Mr. and Mr. Cooper, welcome to the Black Friar Inn. We have you booked in room four. Here are your keys; take the stairs to the third floor. Breakfast in the restaurant is included in your room rate and the full menu is available. If you need anything, please make us aware and enjoy your stay."

"Thank you," they said as they picked up their bags and made their way to the stairs and up to their room.

When they arrived at their room, Kieran took the bag off Cory's shoulder and set both bags down in the hall before opening the door, sweeping Cory off his feet, and carrying him into the room to deposit him on the queen-sized bed. He grabbed their bags from the hall and toed the door shut. A stunned Cory lay on the bed, watching as a dominant Kieran moved toward him. Kieran's movement made Cory shiver as if he was watching a wolf stalking its prey or its mate. Kieran climbed up over Cory so his new husband was pinned to the bed by his weight. He proceeded to claim Cory's mouth in a deep kiss, which melted his lover into the mattress. Cory gave over everything to Kieran, letting him claim Alpha status.

Kieran broke the kiss and sat back, his ass resting on Cory's hips with his knees keeping Cory's arms pinned to his side. His silver-eyed gaze locked with Cory's amber eyes and bore into his soul, letting the older man understand who was in charge. Cory raised his head, exposing his neck in the traditional wolf sign of submission, and Kieran leaned down and sucked a hickey on his husband's neck, marking his territory. Moving enough to begin undressing his husband, Kieran peeled away Cory's shirt, exposing the beautiful sculpted chest, furred with its firm pectorals and erect nipples, which he leaned down and licked before taking the left one between his teeth and chewing lightly, eliciting moans of pleasure from his lover. He kissed his way across Cory's chest to the other nipple, which received the same treatment and drew forth more moans of pleasure. Knowing Cory wouldn't move, Kieran rose up and slid off the bed to divest Cory of his shoes, socks, pants, and underwear, leaving his glorious body naked. Kieran undressed himself before licking his way up Cory's left leg to nuzzle into his crotch and lick and suck on his lover's furry balls and tease the tip of his cock before the object of his attention filled with blood and lifted the object of his attention away to lie on Cory's firm stomach. Kieran returned his oral attention to Cory's balls, watching and listening as his lover tried to hold himself still as he moaned his passion at the attention his husband was lavishing on him. After spit soaking Cory's balls, Kieran licked his way up his lover's hard and thick shaft to capture the throbbing cock in his mouth as he slicked his fingers by stroking Cory's saliva soaked balls. Those slick fingers stroked down across Cory's furry taint into his ass crack to tease his hole until the muscle opened to admit first one finger, followed by two fingers, and after much teasing and edging Cory's hole, swallowed three of Kieran's fingers. Cory was begging between moans for Kieran to claim him.

"Please, babe, I can't take any more teasing. Please, I want you inside me. I need your cock buried in me."

"I'll decide when I'm ready to claim you, Mr. Corwin Cooper. I'm not done making this incredible body moan and ride the edge. You're not ready to be claimed yet, not while you can still string together full sentences. Only when your mind shuts down and you can't speak will I consummate this marriage."

True to his word, Kieran drove Cory to the edge of spending again and again until Cory couldn't speak at all, let alone string a sentence together. Drenched in sweat and pre-cum, Cory couldn't even plead with his eyes for Kieran to take him. Kieran stood and retrieved a condom and lube from his bag. He slicked his cock, rolled on the condom coated with lube, before pulling a rubbery Cory across the bed so his ass rested on the edge of the bed. With his legs lifted to resting on Kieran's shoulders, Kieran slid his hard cock into the exposed ass. As soon as the head of his cock stroked over Cory's abused prostrate, Kieran regarded his husband as he blew a massive load across his abs and furry chest. So hyped up was Kieran, the spams of Cory's ass on his cock had him filling the condom in only a few strokes. When his own orgasm subsided, Kieran slid gently out of his lover's ass. He picked Cory up and resettled his lover on the bed before going to the bathroom, cleaning himself up before returning with a warm damp cloth and cleaning up Cory. Once he'd rinsed off the washcloth, Kieran returned to the bed and curled up beside Cory, and drew his limp lover into his body, resting Cory's head on his chest and wrapping his arm around Cory. He stroked the sweat-damp hair back from Cory's forehead and kissed him on the forehead before they both drifted off to sleep.

Around six o'clock, the alarm on Kieran's phone went off, waking both young men from their long nap. Cory tried to snuggle back in against Kieran's chest, but his husband wouldn't let him.

"Wolf, time to get up, shower, and get something for dinner."

"Not hungry. I'm too worn out to move."

Cory's stomach chose to gurgle its own opinion on the matter of food. He groaned and with reluctance, sat up.

"I'm still as limp as a wet noodle. I did not realize what I was getting myself into when I decided to marry you. Where did my virgin lover learn such a skill?"

"Internet porn. I figured I needed to learn something to keep you interested in me once we were married."

"I will never lose interest in you, love. I never imagined being kept on the verge of orgasm for so long. I don't think I'll be able to come again anytime soon."

"Oh, I think you'll be surprised how many orgasms I can pull out of you over the next couple of days."

"You might want to wait until I write a will before you try and fuck me to death." Cory chuckled as he rose.

Kieran smiled at his husband and wrapped him in a hug before ushering them both into the bathroom to get cleaned up. Kieran reached up and undid the clasp holding the chain, which bound his hair at the nape of his neck. Flexing his shoulders, Cory caught a glimpse of the large bruise on his neck from Kieran claiming his territory. Kieran moved behind him and wrapped his arms around Cory's waist as he rested his chin on Cory's shoulder, tracing the mark he'd left with his tongue, and let a trickle of Silver magic flow over the spot. Kieran smiled. While Silver magic couldn't heal, the magic aided the body's natural processes; the bruise now appeared to be days old instead of only a few hours. Their eyes locked in the mirror, and Cory grinned as he wove the fingers of his left hand into those of Kieran's left hand. He leaned his head back on Kieran's shoulder as his husband licked across his neck and shoulder. Amazing how good letting go and trusting someone else to make the decisions for a while was. He shivered as Kieran's teeth took hold of his earlobe and nibbled the flesh to get his attention.

"You're thinking instead of enjoying, Wolf."

"Only about how wonderful letting my husband make all the decisions for a while is."

"We'll make all the important decisions together. Time to get in the shower, clean up, get dressed, and go down to the restaurant for dinner."

"Okay you'll have to let go for a moment so you can start the shower while I get our kits."

"Oh, who's becoming a feisty pup now?" Kieran chuckled into Cory's ear as he let him go and ducked as Cory laughed and swung at him.

"I'll show you feisty, Mr. Oisín-Cooper." Cory mock lunged at Kieran and slipped out to get their shower kits while Kieran turned and got the shower going.

Cory laughed at how playful Kieran had become. Before he got their kits, Cory picked outfits out of their luggage and laid them out on the bed. While in the bedroom, Cory experienced a tingle of energy all over his body and shivered when he glimpsed the condom Kieran had used glowing silver where the used item hung on the lip of the trashcan. What Cory failed to spot was the small puddle at the bottom of the trashcan also glowed silver where small drips from the tip of the condom pooled. He padded back into the bathroom to gaze at a wet Kieran attempting to wash his hair without, Cory suspected, resorting to magic. Cory stepped into the shower and took over washing Kieran's more than waist-length hair. Kieran sighed and moaned as Cory's fingers worked magic along his scalp and neck. If not for the fact Cory refused to let him cut his hair, Kieran would be tempted to have his hair cut down to a short style.

"However did you manage to wash all this hair before I came along, love?"

"I admit I cheated and used magic. Not how I should be using Silver magic, but I bind the dirt to the shampoo and bind the shampoo to the water and let soap and dirt flow away down the drain." Kieran peered over his shoulder at Cory. "I enjoy having you wash my hair though. You find all these magic spots on my scalp and neck, and the tension flows away."

"I love washing your hair and your body. I can't get enough of being able to touch you. You are made to fit against me."

"I think the same way about how we fit together, Wolf. You came into my life when you did so you would catch me and put me back together when I fell apart."

"I haven't seen you fall apart yet, babe. You're strong, but I will be here to catch you should you fall, and I will hug all the pieces back together. Let's get finished in here and go downstairs so we can eat. I want to walk on the beach in the moonlight with you after dinner."

Kieran turned and embraced Cory. Cory experienced a strong tingle along his skin, which signaled that Kieran had used Silver magic on both of them. He did seem cleaner than he'd ever been before and shot his lover a puzzled glance as Kieran reached behind him and turned off the water.

"All clean. Magic is useful when you're in a hurry; the spell even exfoliates for a deep clean." Kieran grinned and grabbed a towel, proceeding to dry Cory and himself.

They padded out into the bedroom area and dressed in the outfits Cory picked out. For Kieran, a dark blue polo shirt—this brought out the almost blue highlights in his hair—khaki shorts, and leather sandals. Cory drew on a green polo shirt, khaki shorts, and tan boat shoes. Neither young man wore underwear. Cory grabbed his wallet, room key, and phone, and slipped them into his pockets before doing the same for Kieran. Hand in hand, they left the room and descended to the Friar's Pub on the first floor of the inn. They found a table toward the back of the pub and settled in. Cory's confidence waivered a little when confronted with a menu of mostly seafood dishes he'd never experienced before.

"Relax, the food isn't going to eat you. Will you let me order for us both?" Kieran asked.

"Yeah, I'll let you order for us. This is beyond me. Seafood back home is fried catfish or crawdads."

"Yeah, neither of those is seafood. You're on the coast, so let me introduce you to real seafood."

The waiter arrived in a moment. Kieran glanced up at him, his eyes shining silver in his amusement at Cory's idea of what seafood was.

"Welcome to the Friar's Pub. I'm your server, Friar Tim. What can I get for you guys?" he asked.

"Two bowls of cioppino and a bottle of Pinot Noir. We're celebrating." Kieran's voice took on the same thick Maine accent as their waiter.

"So, what are you celebrating, guys?" Tim asked as he jotted down their order.

"We got married today." Kieran beamed as he captured Cory's left hand across the table so their matching gold rings caught the waiter's attention.

"Well, congratulations, guys. I'll be back with your order in a few minutes." He turned and headed off to the kitchen.

"You're showing off, babe. Your accent got so thick, following along got difficult in places. What is cioppino?"

"Cioppino is a hearty seafood stew, full of mussels, clams, scallops, crab, and fish. Trust me, the Friar's Pub is famous for their cioppino." Kieran's Maine accent vanished while he talked with Cory.

Tim returned with their order a few minutes later and set the steaming bowls of stew in front of each of them with care before breaking the seal on the wine and pouring a splash in Kieran's glass for him to sample. Taking a sip, Kieran let the red wine swirl around his tongue for a moment before swallowing and nodding his head in approval for Tim to pour two glasses. Once the wine was poured, Tim went off to check on his other customers, leaving the guys to dine in peace. Kieran eyes were on Cory as he dug in and tried the cioppino, waiting to find out what his reaction would be. The hearty combination of flavors washed over Cory's taste buds, and after swallowing, he smiled at Kieran. They sat and ate; looking at each other with all the love they had for each other. When they were finished, Tim came and cleared their dishes, and checked to discover if they wanted dessert.

"Thank you, but we'll pass on dessert, Tim. If you'll bring the check, we'll be good," Kieran told the young waiter.

Tim left with the dirty dishes and returned a short while later with the folder containing the check, which he placed in front of Kieran before going to check on another customer. When Kieran opened the folder, he was surprised to find a note inside instead of a bill. He held the note up for Cory to read as well.

"Congratulations on your wedding. Another couple has paid for your meal. They wish you the best as you start your new life together. The Management."

"Wow, how sweet of this other couple. I didn't think we did anything to attract a lot of attention," Kieran said as he slipped a twenty-dollar bill into the folder as a tip for their waiter and slipped the note into his pocket.

Cory and he left their table and headed outside to walk down to the harbor and the beach.

Kieran and Cory stood out on the public pier overlooking the ocean, enjoying each other's company and the cool ocean breeze. Cory's gaze swept across the pier and spotted a tourist type sign mounted on a railing. Taking Kieran's hand, he tugged his husband over to the wayside sign. Cory was amazed to discover they were actually inside a huge national park.

"I didn't realize all this was a national park, Kieran."

"Well, the town isn't part of the park but most of the land around here is, including where the compound is part of Arcadia National Park. The park is close to forty-eight thousand acres in size."

"Wow, this park has a lot of land," Cory said as he pulled Kieran against his chest and hugged him tight.

"Yeah, the park is big. We can get the tour of the islands out in the bay, which are part of the park, tomorrow along with the whale watching tour, or if the weather is good and the tides are at reasonable times of the day, we might cross the land bridge over to Bar Island and spend the time between low tides out on the island's beach."

"We have time to do both before either your dad or your uncle comes to pick us up to take us back out the compound."

"I'm sure if we talk to the front desk clerk we can extend our stay in town a few days, so we don't have to cram everything into a couple of days."

"Don't you need to do more training? And what about the plans for our handfasting?"

"Training can wait, Wolf, and as for planning our handfasting, Grams is in control, so everything is well in hand. All we need to do is come up with any personal vows we might want to make. No, the only thing I still need to do is travel over toward Bangor to the Belle family estate and deal with Grandmother and the rest of the Matriarchs."

"I'm happy to stay in town longer then, Kieran."

"Lets go down to the beach and walk along the water's edge."

CHAPTER EIGHTEEN

A few hours after their return to the compound, Kieran and Cory got cleaned up before heading up to the main house to have dinner with the rest of the family. Kieran and Cory went along the pathways, which led to the back of the house and in through the kitchen gardens to the kitchen proper. Líadáin was delighted to find both boys in her kitchen after their absence and put them to work shelling peas for dinner. She did a scan of Cory while the boys worked and stopped them both.

"I realize you're married and monogamous boys, but did you give into temptation during your honeymoon and have unprotected sex?"

"Grams?" Kieran was shocked by his grandmother's blunt question. "No, we used condoms every time, especially when I was entering Cory. Why? What's happened?"

"Our *mac tíre óg* here has no trace of Ebony magic left in his bloodstream. He's flooded with Silver magic. Do you have any of the condoms you took with you left?"

"Yes, ma'am, we put what was left back in Kieran's kit when we packed to come home from the Black Friar," Cory replied.

"*Mo stór*, go back to your place and bring me the condoms that are left. I have a theory about what might have happened."

Kieran sped from the house and raced back to their cabin, taking every shortcut to speed his journey. Cory sat dumbfounded at the worktable in Líadáin's kitchen until she prodded him to action.

"Keep shelling those peas, *mac tíre óg*. When Kieran gets back, we will have our answers to how your transformation was accelerated, and I suspect we'll also learn who the culprit was. Meanwhile, those peas aren't going to shuck themselves, so get busy."

"Yes, ma'am."

Kieran raced in through the front door of the cabin and headed up the stairs into the master bedroom where he collided with his father as the man emerged from the master bath, condom packets in hand. Guilt spread across Kellen's face at being caught red-handed. Kieran regained his physical balance while his emotional balance was still off kilter.

"Dad! What the hell are you doing here and why are you stealing condoms from our place?"

"Ugh, you caught me. I've got a hot date tonight, and I'm all out."

"You do realize, Dad, you're a horrible liar. Grams wants those so she can find out how and by whom Cory's blood transformation was accelerated, but I don't think I'll have to wait for Grams to work her magic on them to find the answer."

"No, you won't, Son. I pricked holes in them and put a tiny Silver magic spell on them, which allowed your loads to pass thorough but not Cory's. I wanted you to have the happiness your uncle didn't get. Now you and Cory can have all the raw sex you want without ever having to worry about accidents damaging your magic the way Brom's was damaged."

Kieran's anger flashed silver in his eyes, and Silver magic ignited around his hands and formed a binding spell around his father. Kellen attempted to break the spell, but to his surprise, he found he couldn't.

"While I love you dearly, Father, I cannot believe the lengths you and Gramps are going to, trying to force me to fit your stupid prophecy. I can't believe after you and Gramps promised to leave us be that you would deliberately put us at risk." Kellen was struggling to breath as Kieran's anger tightened the binding spell around him. "Luckily for us, Cory's Ebony magic was already bound and weakened by his father's Sapphire magic or this would have been disastrous. Come on, let's get back up to the main house, so you can confess to Grams and Cory."

Kellen groaned when Kieran loosened the spell enough that he could follow Kieran back to the kitchen of the main house. Kellen was forced to stand, sheepishly looking at his mother like he was a naughty schoolboy as he confessed his role in Cory's transformation. With a look from Grams, Kieran dropped the binding spell on his father once the man's confession was out in the open.

"Kellen Kieran Oisín, I am so cross with you. Do you realize how much danger you put the boys in?"

"No, Mother. I wanted them to have the freedom to love each other fully without worrying about whether or not they were going to ruin Kieran's magic. I wanted Kieran to have his shifter and love him completely, in all the ways Brom couldn't love his."

"If Cory had not been as far along in his transformation, you might have killed him or Kieran. Lucky for everyone, I reinforced the failing binding spell on Cory's shifter genes. I can't predict what will happen since his blood carries only Sapphire and Silver magic. I can't foresee whether he'll shift or not. So you will keep an eye on these boys for me, Kellen."

"Yes, Mother."

"One more thing. None of us will mention this to anyone else, especially my husband or my other son."

The three men in the kitchen nodded their agreement, and Kellen beat a hasty retreat while Kieran and Cory returned to helping get dinner ready. Once they prepared everything to be cooked, Líadáin sent Kieran off to the living room to hang out with the rest of the men. Kieran entered the living room and was swept into fierce hugs by his uncle and grandfather, while Kellen held back.

"Okay what's the occasion for all the hugging?" Kieran asked as Uncle Brom released him from the hug.

As if Kieran's question triggered a response, Cory and Grams came in each carrying an armload of gifts.

"Happy Birthday, Kieran," everyone shouted.

"Oh, wow, I can't remember the last time anyone celebrated my birthday. Last year, I tested to become a full tracker. Thank you." Kieran turned and was wrapped in Cory's arms. Kieran kissed his husband. "I'm betting you're behind all this, Wolf."

"Well, partly, but I had Grams help me. I needed her help to get everything ready while we were off on our honeymoon. She told me you hadn't had a real birthday party in years, and I wanted to do something special."

Cory pulled Kieran over to the couch and settled in with Kieran resting against him as their family piled gifts around Kieran's feet. Cory reached to the top of the pile and handed Kieran a small gift-wrapped in bright paper.

"This one is from me, babe. Uncle Brom helped me make the pendant, but this is from my heart."

Kieran unwrapped the gift with care to find a black velvet jewelry box. Opening the box, he found a pendant shaped in the form of two wolves running side by side, one amber-eyed, the other diamond-eyed. The beautiful but imperfect forms of the figures told Kieran his uncle did the metal pour for the process while Cory created the actual wax pieces and the mold used to make the pendant.

"This is beautiful, Wolf. Would you put this on me?"

Cory took up the silver pendant, and everyone discovered he didn't flinch from the metal anymore. He pushed Kieran's hair out of the way, put the chain around Kieran's neck, and fastened the clasp. When the pendant was in place, Kieran turned far enough to be able to kiss his husband once again.

"Thank you, Wolf."

"You're welcome. Now you have lots of presents to open."

Kieran dove into the pile of presents like he was ten years old. The expression of joy on his face lit the room. In the midst of his excitement, Kieran plunked one of the bows from his presents on Cory's chest and mock whispered, "I'll save this present for later."

The family erupted in laughter, and Cory blushed a deep crimson. Once all the presents were opened, the family adjourned to the dining room for dinner and birthday cake. When everyone was groaning from how full they were, the family retired to the living room and were sitting down to relax when Kieran's phone rang with a tone he'd set but never expected to ring.

"Who in the world is calling you at this time of night, and what is with the horrible ring tone, Kieran?" Grams asked.

"The tone is howler monkeys and the bigger surprise the caller is Grandmother Belle."

"I didn't even realize she had your cellphone number," Kellen said.

"Actually, I think I left the number with Great-Aunt Desdemona on the off chance the rest of the Matriarchs might decide to overrule Grandmother. Well, I'd better play the game and answer her call," Kieran said, putting the phone on speaker as he answered.

"Huntress-emeritus, how may I be of service?" Kieran's voice almost broke.

Cory and the rest of the family beheld the strong, handsome young man, who was husband, son, nephew, and grandson transform for a moment into the frightened hesitant boy he'd been in one spoken line. Cory wrapped Kieran in his arms to lend him his strength. Bolstered by Cory's presence and the love of the rest of his family, Kieran drew his resolve back together and waited for his grandmother's reply.

"Your year is almost up, Tracker Kieran. The time has come for you to return home and resume your duties to this house."

"To which of my sisters do I report, Huntress-emeritus?"

"You will report to myself and to the Council of Matriarchs, Tracker Kieran. All your sisters failed the test."

"I shall return home and present myself as Hunter-candidate Kieran in a weeks time, Honored Grandmother."

"The Council does not choose to give you such status boy. You will respect your elders in the proper fashion."

Everyone in the room caught the ice and derision in the tone of the woman's voice when she called Kieran boy. Kieran's tone as he replied should have frozen the entire compound and the old woman on the other end of the line.

"The time has come, Honored Grandmother, for the Council to respect me. The fact remains whether this Council chooses to recognize me or not, I am the last child of the last Huntress of the House of Beauty, which makes me the candidate for the test, regardless of my gender. I will be addressed as such until after the test."

"I'm impressed you developed a spine, boy. Come before the Council by the end of the week, and we will decide your standing in the House of Beauty."

"My father and I will arrive at the end of the week, Honored Grandmother, please make sure our quarters in Mother's suite are ready and waiting for our arrival."

"Do not presume to dictate to me, boy. You and your father will stay where I choose to put you. Until such time, Tracker Kieran, you will respect the Council's and my orders."

"As always, Huntress-emeritus, I am the Council's servant. A pleasant day to you, Honored Grandmother."

Kieran disconnected the call before his grandmother said anything more. He leaned back into Cory's embrace and let out a deep sign of relief as he tossed his phone on the coffee table. Cory hugged him tight and nuzzled into his neck.

"Well, as usual, a pleasant conversation. Interesting to note the old battle axe didn't thaw out any over the last thirty years," Grams said as she rose to go get beverages.

"I should come with you, babe. We can face her together."

"I love you, Wolf, and I want to take you with me, but you wouldn't last five minutes in the harpy's lair. I need to do this on my own, even Dad isn't going to be able to enter the Council chambers with me."

"You will need everything we can give you, Kieran, including the full powers of the Silver Witch. In two nights, your father and I will conduct the ritual to transfer the power and title of Silver Witch to you," Gramps said.

"But I didn't cast my personal energy into the barrier spells here to earn my place as an heir to your power, Grandfather."

"You, Cory and Brom will perform the ritual tomorrow at noon."

"Cory? Gramps, you're often coming up with bad ideas, and this is one of them. You realize exposing him to so much Silver magic at once will cause him harm."

"Kieran, your grams is a wise lady, but I can read your husband's aura from here, and he no longer possesses even a trace of Ebony magic in his system. He is the other half of your soul, so he should be part of these rituals as well. You will need him by your side when the time comes."

"If Cory's participation is what you require, he'll be part of the ritual. We'll meet Uncle Brom in the clearing at the center of the compound tomorrow before noon."

"Take the family grimoire with you tonight, Kieran. You will need to read up on the barrier spell and how to merge your power in with all the power of your ancestors," Kellen said.

"Okay, this is a lot to take in, so I think Cory and I will call an end to the evening. I will grab the grimoire on the way out. Thank you all for making this the best birthday ever."

Kieran and Cory hugged everyone and gathered up all the presents into a couple of bags Grams provided them. On the way out of the main house, Kieran detoured into his grandfather's library and crossed to the lectern, which held the Oisín family grimoire. The massive tome held every spell, potion, and history notes ever learned by the family from the time before the ancient war. Some of the languages in the book had been dead for millennia, while others were in such ancient dialects they were hard to comprehend. Kieran touched the book's cover and jumped back as the grimoire glowed before bursting open and flipping to a beautiful illuminated page of a man in silver armor battling a dark, undefined figure. Written in a language Kieran couldn't read was a passage that glowed with importance. Cory moved to stand behind Kieran and peer over his shoulder.

"Is this the prophecy, babe?"

"I'm not sure, Wolf. I can't read the language this passage is written in. Taking a wild guess, I think this is the ancient prophecy about the Silver Hunter. I will need to cast a translation spell on this page to be able to read what's written here."

Kieran closed the book, and the grimoire shrank in size to fit into one of the bags they carried.

"Well, at least the book doesn't make you carry around the deluxe family size," Cory joked.

"Yeah, if the grimoire stayed full-size, I would strap the thing to my handy pack wolf's back for him to carry home for me," Kieran said from behind one of his brilliant smiles.

"You do realize, Mr. Birthday Boy, you're still going to receive the traditional birthday spankings. How much they sting is up to your attitude." Cory's grin carried a huge trace of hungry wolf.

Kieran wisely decided to pick up the bag containing the grimoire to carry back to their cabin. The young men returned to their cabin and put away Kieran's gifts. Kieran set up the grimoire on a desk in the small office off the kitchen. Once in place, the book returned to its normal size and flipped open to the page containing the prophecy.

"Somehow, I get the idea the grimoire isn't going to let me ignore the old prophecy. I don't get what the book wants me to understand about the subject. The language is so old I'm not sure I can find a translation spell in the book that would work."

Kieran glared at the ancient book, almost as if willing the book to speak to him.

"Leave the prophecy for the night, babe. You didn't collect your last present yet."

Kieran turned to find Cory standing in the doorway of the kitchen with his shirt off, his jeans unbuttoned, and the zipper pulled down enough to reveal the top of his blond pubic hair and barely containing his swelling cock. Between the front door and the kitchen, Cory ditched his shoes, leaving him standing in the doorway barefoot. Kieran's eyes went to his lover's fur-covered chest and down the washboard abs to the invitation of the open jeans. With the grace of a hunting cat, Kieran pounced and locked lips with Cory. Tongues dueled for dominance until Kieran gave into his desire and let Cory assume control. The next moments made Kieran glad his current shirt didn't number among his favorites. The sound of ripping fabric was all the warning he received as Cory tore the shirt off him. His jeans soon pooled around his ankles, and he managed to toe off his shoes before finding himself hoisted over Cory's broad shoulders, being carried to their bedroom.

On the way up the stairs, Cory administered Kieran's twenty-two birthday spanks as they reached the massive bed. Cory shrugged Kieran off his shoulders to the bed, where he landed face first, leaving his crimson glowing ass exposed to Cory's viewing pleasure. As Kieran reached back to rub his ass, Cory caught his hands and held them away from his husband's body.

"You keep your hands on the bed, mister. I'll tend to your ass in a moment. You passed up your chance to be in control of how you received your gift downstairs. I'm the boss tonight." Cory's voice was deep and carried the edge of a growl, which never failed to drive Kieran mad with lust.

"I promise I'll behave, Mr. Oisín-Cooper," Kieran purred back.

"You can bet your sweet ass you'll behave, Mr. Oisín-Cooper," Cory growled back.

Kieran listened as Cory's jeans hit the floor before wet warmth and the bristle of facial hair began working over the red globes of Kieran's ass, working their way toward the split between the firm mounds. Soon, firm hands gently spread the flesh as the probing tongue established its presence by swiping along the exposed flesh and returning to pay particular attention to the rosy hole at the center. Teasing the pucker flesh, the firm tongue worked its way inside to the obvious pleasure of its owner as evidenced by the deep moans. Soon, Kieran was a molten puddle of flesh as Cory slid his finger in to massage the prostate as his tongue teased the flesh of Kieran's perineum. Kieran did his best to stay still beneath Cory's provocative activities. Much too soon, he found himself moaning he was going to come.

Cory stopped all his actions and let Kieran cool down from the edge before flipping him over, exposing his husband's raging erection. Cory slid up Kieran's body, making sure his chest hair touched all Kieran's most sensitive spots, until their cocks were rubbing next to each other and their chests rose and fell in a rhythm. Leaning down, he brushed his beard along the side of Kieran's neck before licking his way up long the exposed flesh to his lover's ear, which he drew into his mouth and nibbled on the lobe, driving Kieran mad with lust. Taking some pity on his whimpering husband,

Cory moved his head so their lips lined up, and he clamped down in a fierce kiss, which threatened to suck the air out of Kieran's lungs. When breathing became a desperate necessity, Kieran found the one spot Cory was most ticklish and used the spot to break the kiss.

"Understanding we promised to love each other until death do us part, Wolf, don't you think we should save this kind of killer kiss for when we're old and gray?"

"Sorry, babe, you have me so turned on I couldn't help myself."

"Well I've got a better idea. Why don't you put your raging hard cock to good use and make love to your husband?"

"I like your thinking. Do you think we're safe making love to you flesh to flesh?"

"Gramps confirmed you're free of all Ebony magic. I think we're safe to go without the condom, if you're comfortable about doing so."

"Better play safe a while longer. I'd rather claim you as my mate under the power of your ritual when we're sure everything is safe."

Cory reached across the bed to grab the lube and a condom from the nightstand, and Kieran took advantage of his stretch to latch his mouth and teeth gently on Cory's right nipple to tease his lover. Cory lightly swatted Kieran away before hooking his arms under his lover's legs and hoisting them up over his shoulders. Slicking his cock, he slipped the rubber on before slicking the condom as well. Cory rose up and slid his cock into Kieran's ass slow and deep; he set up a gentle rhythm, intending to make the evening last. He leaned forward, bending Kieran's legs back until he locked lips and kissed his husband as they made love.

"Happy Birthday, babe."

"Thank you, Wolf. This is the best birthday I've ever had."

"I plan to make them all special from now on."

Cory rose up and adjusted Kieran's legs so they were wrapped around his waist and resumed his thrusting, speeding up as he drew closer to the edge of orgasm. Soon, Kieran's breathing matched Cory's as they reached climax together. Kieran's load splattered both young men's chests as Cory's filled the condom. Careful to make sure he had a grip on the condom Cory withdrew his spent cock from Kieran's ass and collapsed beside his husband. They kissed before Kieran found a spot on Cory's chest, which wasn't sticky with spent cum, and rested his head on the spot. Cory's fingers found their home in Kieran's hair, stroking the spot at the base of his neck, which always relaxed his lover. Despite all their relaxing activities, Kieran's neck muscles were already beginning to tense up.

"You're thinking deep thoughts already."

"I'm sorry. Thinking about dealing with my Grandmother Belle later this week, she's never been an easy person to be in the same room as. I'm pretty sure I always cower or give deference to her. I'm not sure how to oppose her and earn her respect without blowing a hole through the council chamber or one of my great-aunts."

"Are you sure you don't want me to come with you? What if we redirected their focus on to your shifter-stock husband?"

"Bright Mother, the thought of the cascade of heart attacks lightens my heart. I want to show you where I grew up, but now is not the time. I need to make them accept me as the Hunter-candidate, and as much as I love you, Wolf, I won't be able to convince them if I walk into the council chamber with you and Billy in tow."

"What's Billy got to do with all this?"

"If I take you as my husband, I will need to take Billy as my dark shifter and claim a title as yet unearned. I would be forced to walk into the House of Beauty as the Silver Hunter. No, for now, I need to be Tracker Kieran, petitioning for my place as Hunter-candidate."

"Okay, we'll do this your way. You must approach the Alpha of your family, showing enough respect to keep her from guessing you're challenging to take the pack away from her."

"Something along those lines. Let's go take a shower. I want to cuddle properly and not get all sticky. Besides we need to get some sleep. We're going on a long hike and working a long day tomorrow."

"The barrier spell?"

"Yes, I need to read up on the spell if the grimoire will let me turn the pages."

"Is the book alive, babe?"

"To tell you the truth, Wolf, I wouldn't be surprised if the book was alive. I think the grimoire has been the focus of so much high-level magic over the centuries, perhaps the thing has developed an awareness."

"Let's shower; then, we'll go check out your living book."

****

Hours later, Kieran rose in frustration as the grimoire refused to allow him to turn the page from the prophecy. He wanted to hurl the book into a fire, but suspected the tome was protected from such actions. Pacing across to the kitchen, Kieran snarled when he reached the fridge and started reaching for yet another soda. He was wired on caffeine enough. He rounded on the book, snarling in rage, Silver magic flaring in his eyes.

"What is in this fucking prophecy you want me to understand, you stupid book? I don't want to be the blasted Silver Hunter. I want to be Kieran Oisín-Cooper and go live on a godforsaken farm far away from the never-properly-cursed House of Beauty. To be honest with you, book, I don't even want to be the heir to the Silver Witch. I want to be a normal gay guy. Where is the spell in your pages for granting such a wish?"

To Kieran's surprise, the book slammed shut, and a ghost-like figure emerged from the grimoire. Silver magic swirled around Kieran's hands as he raised them to ward of the ghost.

"For someone who doesn't want his Silver magic, you're pretty quick to raise magic for defense."

"Who are you?"

"I don't suppose you would buy the genie of the lamp here to grant you three wishes," the figure teased.

"You're in the wrong book of wonder tales. I think Aladdin lives about five thousand miles east of here."

"Well, at least you still possess a sense of humor. I figured humor died out of my sister's line a long time ago."

"You're Beauty's brother, the one who became the first male Silver Witch."

"Yes, Kieran Samuel Belle Oisín-Cooper, my what a mouthful. I think I'll call you Kieran. I am or I used to be Johan Kaufmann, and like you, I was destined to be the Silver Hunter. I'm the one who should have slain the Beast; instead, I acted the coward and let my little sister go and face the monster."

"So I'm not the first person cursed to fulfill this prophecy. Is this some sort of reoccurring curse or did everyone before me chicken out?"

"I guess you would say I chickened out. Most of those called to do the job never answered the call for one reason or another, mostly because they grew up repressed by the women of my sister's line. Ten generations ago, a glimmer of hope appeared when the first man became the Hunter of the House of Beauty."

"He didn't fit the requirements, did he? Wouldn't take a shifter for a mate for starters, even though several were offered to him."

"Well, I gather the Historians of the House of Beauty still keep two sets of books."

"Yes, and Great-Uncle Jonas showed me the 'this is the true account' set regarding the male hunter. If I'm going to deal with this prophecy, I need to understand what is in the blasted thing. I can't even begin to read this language."

"Let me translate the prophecy for you. You might want to write this down."

From behind him, Cory handed him a pad and pen. Kieran turned and stared at his husband.

"Thanks, Wolf. I'm sorry I woke you."

"I told you we would do this together. I should've realized you couldn't let this go, so I got up when you started shouting at a book. Somehow, I didn't expect a ghost to be answering you back."

"I didn't expect an audio answer either, but here's Johan, Beauty's youngest brother and the first male Silver Witch. Johan, this is my husband, Corwin Samuel Cooper."

"I like how Kieran calls you Wolf. Now do you boys want the translation?"

"Okay, go ahead and translate," Kieran replied.

"When the lines of white do twist and twine, the firstborn of the second son shall of two Houses be. Child of the White Witch thy path doth wind, like the goddess a threefold way, Tracker, Witch, and Hunter thee. A lone journey to the city named for a small stone, leads the Child of Beauty to his soul's mate. From the ever-shifting line of the Ebony beast, shall a never-changing pup's soul bind to your fate? When bound are two souls, which cannot part, 'ware to those who work the dark art. The hour draws nigh to confront the heir of the dark beast. One whose shape shifts shall claw the light to bring on the dark feast. Boundaries of magic and of flesh shall shatter, and white will shift its shape. Hunter in white thy time has appeared, call forth thy mate and thy guard, this fate thou cannot escape. Slender chains of white bind you, yours the mage's burden to bear. Bound or free, only the rising gold shall reveal your fate by its rising glare."

"Okay, this is the usual nonsense of a prophecy." Kieran tossed the pad down in frustration.

"No, babe. This whole thing does seem to point to us. These lines here describe you to a T. You're the firstborn of a second son of one line with Silver magic, and I guess the House of Beauty would be considered a second line with Silver magic."

"Those lines contain the first problem. The prophecy says white, not silver," Kieran said.

"If I might interject. Some of the translations use silver instead of white. We used to debate this back in my day when Silver magic families were more numerous," Johan offered

"So what was our family's position on the matter? Gramps seems to side with the silver translation," Kieran asked.

"Silver has always been our position, given no one's working white magic," Johan replied.

"Okay, so for argument's sake, let's go with silver instead of white. Now I can relate to the prophecy talking about me. I guess this part about a never-changing pup might refer to Cory since our souls are bound together," Kieran mused aloud.

"The heir to the dark beast must be the Alpha who's taken over the pack in the forest on the Belle estate and ordered the murder of your sisters," Cory offered.

"Yes, now I must take the test, which means facing him in combat. These lines about the Hunter in silver calling forth his mate and his guard sound similar to another verse I learned elsewhere about a dark shifter on his left and a light shifter on his right—or was the line an ebony shifter and a silver shifter? Those don't work either, because silver shifters don't exist," Kieran explained.

"What's this one about boundaries of magic and flesh shattering and silver shifting its shape? Would the passage mean I'm eventually going to shift since I still have the genes for shifting, even though all the Ebony magic is gone from my blood?" Cory asked.

"I never considered your genes. I suppose we might interpret the passage in such a way. All right, I can't wriggle out of the prophecy. Johan, I need every drop of power I can get. First, I need the barrier spell. Time to tinker with the spell, we need to separate the spell from the bloodline and tie the barrier to an object each Silver Witch candidate can add power to." Kieran's voice now held determination.

Cory withdrew to the kitchen to make a light breakfast and coffee for himself and Kieran, while Kieran and the ghost of Johan read over the barrier spell. Kieran began making notes on the spell and adapting changes to refocus the power from the living bloodline to an artifact to be charged by each new generation. Afterward, he focused on the ritual for becoming the Silver Witch's formal heir.

"Well, this one I'm going to have to do by all the traditional methods, because Gramps will be in charge, and if I mess up, things will go wrong."

"Yes, this is perhaps the one ritual you cannot change to suit your own style, Kieran," Johan said.

"Thank you for your help, Johan. How do I return you to your rest within the grimoire?"

Johan didn't reply to Kieran's question, and his ghostly presence was gone. Kieran closed the grimoire and made his way into the kitchen where Cory was getting ready to pour two mugs of coffee. He stopped Cory before he poured the first cup and waited while his love set down the pot before he wrapped himself in Cory's arms. They stayed wrapped up in a hug for several moments before Kieran broke the silence.

"I'm sorry, Wolf, but we have to fast for the next couple of days. These spells all call for fasting before they're cast, and I don't understand them well enough to attempt changing them up more than I'm going to. Everyone wants you included in these spells and rituals, so I'm afraid you have to starve along with me. Pure water is all were allowed until after I'm invested as Gramps' heir."

"Okay so forty-eight hours or so of fasting. I think I can survive, babe. What else do I need to be aware of or do?"

"Well, we're going to be spending a lot of time out in the woods naked with Uncle Brom."

"Are you worried I'm going to start drooling over your uncle, babe?"

"Ugh, you're learning to read our bond to well, Wolf."

"Nope, I remember how your sexy uncle is the only thing we've ever fought over. You don't need to worry. We may not have done any fancy rituals—aside from my pledging my faithfulness to you until death does us part when we got married in town—but because your seed has been in me and changed me, our bond is even deeper than you think. I'm your mated partner."

Kieran turned in Cory's arms so they were face to face and drew his husband in for a deep kiss.

"Pack up as much bottled water as you can carry comfortably, Wolf. I'm going to go get the items I need to work with and talk with Uncle Brom about bringing a few items as well. Oh, and grab a couple of towels as well. We have to take a ritual bath at the spring before we begin working magic."

The lovers separated, going to get themselves ready for their day. Kieran filled a backpack with a serious array of magical tools, including the family grimoire. He strapped on his silver sabers and loosely bound his hair with a simple silver clasp. Going back downstairs, he found Cory waiting for him with a daypack filled with bottled water and a pair of towels. Beside Cory was a staff of oak capped at each end with silver, which Kieran recognized as his uncle's work. Cory stood, shouldered the pack, and took up his staff. The lovers kissed one more time before Kieran led them outside where they we're met by not only Uncle Brom, but Kellen and Gramps as well. Kieran was surprised to find his male relatives dressed and ready to go.

"I thought only Uncle Brom was going to go with us to do the barrier spell," Kieran said.

"Brom told us about your innovation to the spell, and we thought our help would make the spell even stronger if we added our power to your new version."

"You're testing me, evaluating if my spell is up to the task of proving me worthy to be the Silver Witch if the need arises. I suppose this happens with every generation, even though Johan didn't say anything about these kinds of tests last night while we worked on the changes."

"Johan? Who is Johan, Son?" Kellen asked, looking puzzled at his son.

Kieran glanced back at his father and grandfather, as puzzled as the two older men.

"The spirit of the grimoire, the first male Silver Witch, the youngest of Beauty's brothers, the guy who didn't take the job as the Silver Hunter. Are you telling me you never interacted with him?"

"I don't think we were ever suppose to interact with him if he was destined to be the Silver Hunter. Neither your father nor I were ever fated to be the Silver Hunter," Gramps replied.

"Freaking awesome. So how about you, Uncle Brom? You're being too quiet on the subject."

Brom swallowed a lump in his throat and tears formed in his silver eyes, which he tried to blink away.

"Only once. He appeared right after I recovered from having my magic ruined by my foolish bout of unsafe sex with a shifter. He said I tried to take on a destiny that belonged to another, and told me I'll recognize the chosen one when he comes crying to me for love and attention. I've been aware of your destiny since you came to me at age ten, *mo stór*."

"Oh, *mo mhúinteoir*, my teacher and beloved uncle, he's right you tried to take on too much." Kieran wrapped his uncle in a fierce hug. "You sacrificed your place as Gramps' heir for a nephew you'd never even met. Why did you think I'm worthy of such a sacrifice?"

"Because you are my little brother's son. I would give anything to keep you from such a destiny, and my own foolish notions of love blinded me."

"Well, I love you dearly, Uncle, ever my wise counsel since I was bawling child of ten. Because of you, I found the strength to face my destiny. Now, we need to get hiking if we're going get to the center of the property with time to set up. This is the last chance to back out or ask questions. Once we leave here, silence must hold until we begin the ritual to cast the new barrier spell."

Kieran paused and glanced at everyone in turn from his grandfather around to his husband. They merely nodded their agreement, and silence settled over the group. Kieran gestured for Brom to lead the way and let his father and grandfather precede Cory and himself. Cory smiled at his husband and fell into place behind him as the group set off single file. Billy popped up and fell in beside Kieran, butting his head against Kieran's hand for attention. Kieran let his hand caress Billy between the ears. Receiving a magical nudge, he paused and bent down to meet Billy's eyes. The boy/wolf nodded his head, licked Kieran in the face, and resumed trotting along beside the group. Kieran rose, resuming his trek with Billy at his side. The spell he was planning on casting played in his mind and shifted form before his mind's eye as Billy's part became clear in the new pattern of the spell. The woods of the Oisín compound were filled with the sounds of wildlife as the men and the wolf made their way to the sacred center of the property. When they reached the edge of the clearing, they stopped to gather as a group. At a gesture from Kieran, they all stripped off their clothes and waited while Kieran entered the clearing with one of his silver sabers bared. Moving to the north, Kieran saluted the giant quartz pillar with his sword before bowing to honor the Guardian of Earth. Proceeding clockwise, Kieran repeated his ritual before each of the other pillars until he once more faced the northern pillar. Here, he raised his arms and the saber above his head, and with a silent cry, released Silver magic to form a dome around the clearing. He moved to the place inside his dome where the outside path met the edge of the dome between North and East. Saluting the dome, he placed his saber at ground level and traced upwards, across, down, and back across to his point of origin. Where the sword cut, the dome faded away, creating a doorway. Kieran bid each member of his party to come forward and challenged each with the tip of his sabre until each nodded his agreement to enter in silence and reverence. In silence, his directed Cory and Billy to the center of the circle as his grandfather, father, and uncle each moved to their favored quarter. Gramps moved to the North as Guide, Kellen to the East as Rover, Brom to the South as Guardian, leaving the West open for Kieran as Hunter, each man representing a facet of the god.

Kieran swept his saber back across the entrance he'd cut and sealed the dome once more before laying his saber across the path to cut a door in case of an emergency. Moving clockwise around the circle, Kieran took up his position in the West. The four men of the Oisín clan raised their hands over their heads and joined their magic in a silent evocation to the goddess and the god to bless their working. Surprising everyone, especially Cory, Billy remained silent despite the outpouring of Silver magic all around him. Kieran merely smiled at his husband and nodded to his family. Each of the Oisín men stepped forward to the center from their quarter of the circle until they were linking hands in a circle around Cory and Billy. The ground shivered a moment, causing Cory and Billy to shift toward Kieran, as a flat stone rose from the ground braced on two pillars of quartz to form an altar. When the altar settled into place, the Silver mages released their circle and waited for Kieran's next instruction.

Wordless, Kieran gestured for them to stay put while he crossed to his saber and reopened the doorway to the outside. He crossed the threshold and gathered up his backpack before returning inside the dome and resealing the doorway. Moving to stand before the altar, Kieran pulled out several items from his backpack and placed them on the altar, the grimoire, a bell, a plate, a chalice, a pair of candles, a silver dagger, a silver flask, and a small silver box. Gramps took the candles and set them into small indentations in the surface of the altar, while Kellen took the plate and the chalice and set them on the center of the altar. Brom picked up the flask and the box, setting them to the side. Kieran set the bell on the opposite side of the altar from the flask and the box. He set the grimoire into a rest at the front of the altar and opened the book to the page containing the ritual for barrier spell, resting the silver dagger in the seam of the book as a bookmark. Still silence reigned over the group as Kieran knelt before the altar and bowed his head in prayer. When Kieran arose, he picked up the flask, twisted of the cap, and poured the contents into the chalice before returning the flask to the altar and taking up the box. Opening the box, he removed a strike anywhere match, which he struck and used to light the candles. Kieran removed a piece of flat bread from the box and placed the bread on the plate. He tore the bread into five pieces and spoke for the first time.

"We are gathered before the goddess and the god to ask their aid in our work. When our working is completed, we shall partake in this offering to the ancient ones."

The Oisín men replied, "So mote it be."

Kieran reached over his shoulder as if reaching for a sword, and when he pulled his arm back, a silver sword gleamed in his hand. He held the sword upright for a moment before setting the blade on the altar.

"This is the sword of my sister Rosalind Belle, who died a huntress of the House of Beauty. This sword will anchor the barrier we craft this day. Cory and Billy, please come here," Kieran, said the last part as he took up the silver dagger. "All magic comes at a price, and every spell must contain a way for the magic to be broken. The barrier, which protects these lands, is meant to keep out shifters, but can be shattered if a shifter transforms from one shape to another within the barrier. Today, we will craft a new barrier, which can only be shattered by the use of an item enchanted by an Ebony mage, whose power is equal to or greater than the power of the Silver

Witch, to shatter this sword. To invoke this power, I need a drop of blood from each of you."

Cory held out his hand, and Billy raised a paw, both of which Kieran swiftly pricked with the point of the dagger. He touched the tip of the dagger to the blade of the sword and began a chant, which his family took up and repeated three times. Power surged and swirled around the domed circle until Kieran drew the power in and took hold of the sword's pommel, directing the power into the sword. Lifting the sword, Kieran slammed the blade point first into the ground in front of the altar, burying the sword to the hilt in the earth.

The spell's power flowed out to the pillars of the circle and sucked away the dome the Oisín men had raised before releasing a sphere of power outwards with the sword at the center. All four Silver mages collapsed to the ground as their power was drawn into the spell in the initial phase before rushing back into them like a surging tide. Brom recovered first, because he was the least powerful of the four men. He prevented Cory from rushing to Kieran's side and touching him.

"Cory, stop. Don't touch him until he starts to come around on his own or you'll kill him. He has to recover his balance with his power, and an outside touch will upset the balance within him."

Kellen and Gramps eventually recovered and sat up. They stood watching as Kieran's body lay twitching from the power surging around and through him. Long minutes passed, and worried expressions grew on the older mages' faces, as Kieran still didn't revive. Before anyone tried to stop him, Billy surged forward and licked Kieran's face, shocking the young mage back to reality. Slowly, he sat up, blinking his eyes back into focus. Kieran glanced around and smiled at his family.

"Well, how did I do with my first major working?"

Cory grabbed him from behind in a tight hug and said, "You scared us all half to death, babe. We feared for you until Billy licked your face and woke you up."

Billy nudged his head into Kieran's chest, and Kieran ruffled his fur from ears to neck.

"So I get woken up by true love's doggie slobber instead of a kiss." Kieran chuckled as he scratched Billy behind his ears.

"Impressive, Grandson. You proved you can cast a spell in the traditional manner, even if you did bend the spell all out of shape while doing the casting. Come, let us partake of the offering to the gods, and give thanks."

Gramps took up the plate and handed each of them a piece of the bread. They all ate, and Kellen took up the chalice and passed the cup around until they all drink from the cup. With some help, Kieran rose on wobbling legs and hobbled over to where his saber lay across the path. The blade was a twisted, darkened wreck. Kieran picked sword up and reverently laid the saber on the altar along with the undamaged twin blade. After extinguishing the candles, Kieran cleaned and packed everything up. With a gesture, Kellen sent the altar back into the ground, taking the sabers as well. The group got dressed, and Cory handed out bottled water to everyone.

"I do not believe this. I lost another set of sabers to magic." Kieran sighed as they left the clearing to return to their cabins.

"We'll forge you a new set after your initiation as heir to the Silver Witch, *mo stór*."

"Thank you, Uncle Brom."

They reached a point on the trail where three separate trails branched off. Brom took the trail to the left, Gramps and Kellen took the path to the right, and Kieran led Cory and Billy along the center path back to their cabin. Cory didn't understand how three paths now existed when on the way in only one existed. Kieran gave him a brief explanation of the magic of the path as they returned to their cabin. The young couple and their wolf arrived back at their cabin and went in to clean up and rest. Cory put the remaining bottled waters back in the fridge to chill before heading upstairs to join Kieran in the shower.

INTERLUDE: THE MASTER WATCHES AND PLOTS

Many miles away, the Ebony mage, who styled himself the Master, awoke from his meditative trance as he experienced the power of Kieran's massive working. He trembled in sudden fear as proof of the existence of at least four Silver mages of vast power hit home. Reaching out with his own dark power, he explored around the edges of the monumental working. Yes, four Silver mages, one old and vastly powerful, two middle aged, one his equal and tied to the old man like an apprentice. The other was damaged in some way; he couldn't tell why, but definitely weaker. The forth proved to be the boy Simms kept promising to deliver to him. The tracker from the House of Beauty, who shouldn't possess magic or at the best a weak one-shot talent, turned out to be related to the other three mages by blood and possessed their talent in full measure. The boy ranked as his equal in power, and the Master trembled as he read the potential for greater power than even the old mage of the group. The boy must be captured and broken before his potential became unlocked. Time to put his apprentice into the field again. His apprentice would make sure Kincaid and his group of ragtag shifters didn't make a mess of the capture of the boy. From his lair, the Master redirected Marissa Holden, the little owl shifter, from her task aiding Kincaid to finding a way to get inside the enemy stronghold and break the barrier spells on the hidden compound. He needed to go down to his vault and check the inventory of enchanted items left over from his predecessor's reign.

The boy's untapped potential troubled the Master. This foe's creative use of magic terrified the Ebony mage in a way not experienced since his time as a slave-apprentice. So much power pulsed in the sword, which held the inner barrier spell in place; the mage didn't think he possessed a single dark object with enough power to break the spell. He would need to merge two or more objects to get the power. Rising, from his bed the Master found his eager new slave-apprentice waiting to serve him. The mage cuffed the boy aside and wrapped his body in the shadow robes he preferred before striding from his bedchamber headed for his library and the vault, which lay beyond. This new slave-apprentice didn't possess a large potential for Ebony magic, but he made a pleasant diversion in bed, and William Harkrider proved his usefulness when he brought his family's enchanted compass in trade for his apprenticeship.

CHAPTER NINETEEN

After an exhausted night's sleep, Kieran woke still snuggled up to Cory and giggled when he caught his husband's stomach growling. Cory groaned as his stomach complained about its empty status. Kieran's fingers began stroking through the hair on his husband's chest, roaming down the abs to skirt along his waist before traveling back up to play with first one nipple and then the other before resuming their teasing travels. A low possessive growl rumbled from the back of Cory's throat as Kieran's fingers slipped below the sheet to wrap around his cock. The gentle tugs took him from soft to stiff in mere moments. His husband's fingers released their grip on his now solid manhood and trailed down to play with his full balls before slipping lower to tease their way back to his hole. Kieran, lying next to him, let his fingers do all the work. Cory realized Kieran was doing everything as if on autopilot, his mind elsewhere.

"Kieran, you're distracted. I can tell your mind is off someplace else."

"I'm sorry, Wolf. I love touching you, and normally, doing so takes my mind off my problems; this time the reverse seems to be happening."

"Talk to me, babe. What's got you distracted from loving your husband?"

"I sense a darkness encroaching on our time together. Those lines of the stupid prophecy we couldn't figure out are nagging at me, Wolf."

"Babe, I don't think trying to figure them out on an empty stomach is a good idea. I understand we can't eat for several hours yet, so why don't we go out back and swim in the lake."

"I guess some sort of physical activity would be a good idea. We've got a couple of hours before we need to join Gramps up at the house for the ritual to tie me into the powers of the Silver Witch."

"Well, if physical activity is what you need, lover," Cory said with a sexy grin.

"After the ritual, Wolf, I promise we can fuck like bunnies in heat."

"No food and no sex. This ritual better be impressive."

"I have no idea, Wolf. The grimoire says the ritual is performed however the current Silver Witch chooses. Considering how much of a traditionalist Gramps is, I would imagine all sorts of crazy prayers and magic gestures."

"Like all the things you did yesterday?"

"Yeah, only about ten times more showy, Wolf. Let's grab our trunks and hit the lake."

The guys got out of bed and crossed the room to the dresser where they rummaged for their swim trunks. Once they were dressed, they grabbed towels and headed downstairs and out the back door of their cabin. The back porch opened on to a long pier, which extended out into the lake. A small fishing boat was tied up at the end of the pier next to a ladder for getting back out of the water. When they got to the end of the pier and had set down their towels, Kieran grab Cory in a fierce hug and kiss as he launched them off the end of the pier and into the icy waters of the lake. He held them both under the water for a moment before breaking the kiss, and with a powerful kick, he sent them to the surface. When they broke the surface, Cory glared at him, which caused Kieran to break out in laughter.

"What's with you and water? Every time we go swimming, you try to drown me."

"Oh no, Wolf. I love watching your reactions when we break the surface. Your inner wolf doesn't like being near this much water, and he sort of surfaces when I dunk you."

"Deep inside you is a part that enjoys toying with a dangerous beast. You're an adrenaline junkie."

"Trust me, Cory, I'm not chasing an artificial high. Being with you charges my batteries in ways I can't begin to express. If I didn't grasp the complexity of my family bloodlines as well as I do, I'd swear shifter blood crept in somewhere way back. I want to howl at the moon, run, and chase you—or be chased by you—through the woods."

"Um, Kieran, I can't keep this from you, even though your Gramps and Dad made me promise never to tell you."

"What are those two up to this time?" Kieran's voice was tinted with annoyance.

"Beauty's prince and the Beast shared a mother who was part shifter. They said her daughter used her one shot of Silver magic to bind the shifter blood in her children so they'd never be able to shift but they'd have all the strength and tracking skills of a shifter."

Silver magic flowed around the young lovers as Kieran raised them on a platform out of the water. He didn't appear angry, but Cory experienced the tension through the bond. He drew Kieran into a hug and turned him so they both stood on the silver platform looking out over the lake. Cory rested his chin on Kieran's shoulder so his beard tickled the side of Kieran's neck.

"I upset you. I shouldn't have said anything, but I think this is the reason for our ability to bond at all, love. The tiny amount of shifter blood in you calls to the massive amounts of shifter blood in me."

"Actually, what you told me explains a lot of things I wondered about over the years, Wolf. I always wondered how the members of the House of Beauty managed to keep up with the shifters we hunted. My tutors said our ability comes from the Silver magic in our veins, but their answer didn't explain why even my non-gifted relatives are able to track shifters so easily."

"I guess even the House of Beauty hid the truth from itself."

"Only one person would have been privy to the truth, Great-Uncle Jonas the family historian. His line kept the history of the House of Beauty from the day Beauty charged her firstborn son with the job until Jonas' death. I always suspected the existence of more secret chronicles hidden away in the archives besides those on the only male hunter."

"Do you think your great-uncle left a clue to where they were hidden?"

"I can only hope he did. He died about a year after Mom did of extreme old age and without a successor. I think he wanted me to be his choice, but I'd already taken the tests and proven I possessed the talent for tracking. All my other male relatives were two young for the task. I can't help but think that under different circumstances, Rosie would have been the Jonas' successor if either Selene or Celeste passed the test and became the Huntress. She was the only one besides me to give the old man more than a passing nod. We used to sit for hours listening to stories from the chronicles when we escaped our lessons." Kieran's voice grew hushed and raspy as he tried to fight his emotions back under control.

"I wish I could have met your sister Rosie. I can tell by the tone in your voice and experience through our bond how special she is to you."

"Rosie was special, Wolf. She would have been the first one to welcome you with open arms, and she would have beat me with whatever she laid her hands on for letting out relationship fade out between Thanksgiving and Christmas."

Cory laughed as a vivid picture of the petit but beautiful and powerful Rosie surged up out of Kieran's mind and across their bond. Kieran's image of a miniature Amazon warrior chasing him with a lamp was too cute. A tear escaped from both of them as Kieran fondly remembered his sister. Sensing his lover was trying hard not to loose control of his emotions, Cory hugged Kieran tighter for a moment before taking advantage of Kieran's distracted thoughts to push him off the platform. The shock of the cold water broke Kieran's concentration, and Cory yelped as he plunged into the water a moment after Kieran went in. Sputtering to the surface, Cory couldn't help but laugh at Kieran's expression this time around, as his lover trod water, trying to get his hair out of his face. The lovers abandoned all serious thoughts and began chasing each other through the water, dunking, groping, and kissing as the mood took them. Eventually, they grew tired and cold, so they climbed out on the pier to dry off and grab some sun. After awhile, Kieran shifted so his head rested on Cory's chest with his arm draped over Cory's waist. Feeling tears drip on his chest along with flashes of grief through their bond, Cory wrapped his arm around Kieran's shoulders and pulled him in tight. They settled into a true Alpha/Alpha partnership, with each of them taking the lead as needed. Knowing his lover needed peace and a quiet release of some of his grief, Cory held him, letting love and contentment flow through their bond while lightly stroking Kieran's hair. They lay in silence until the heat of the day began to get to them.

"Do you want to go for another quick swim or head in and shower, Wolf?" Kieran said as he wiped the last of his tears from his eyes.

"Let's head in, love. I think we've both gotten enough sun for the day. I'll grab us a couple of bottles of water while you go start the shower."

They padded their way back down the pier to the cabin and headed inside, separating in the kitchen as Cory stopped at the refrigerator to grab a couple bottled waters. Kieran continued upstairs into the bathroom to start the shower. The young couple downed their waters before shucking their trunks and stepping into the shower enclosure. Cory took up the shampoo once Kieran had soaked his hair. He soon had his husband moaning in pleasure as he worked up a thick lather and worked his fingers into the scalp and down into the neck muscles. When Kieran backed up against his husband so Cory's cock slipped into the crease of his lover's ass, Cory reached around and killed the hot water. The shock of the sudden cold water snapped Kieran out of his trance and reminded him they couldn't have sex until after the ritual tonight. Kieran restored the hot water for Cory to finish rinsing the shampoo out of his hair before they shut down the shower and dried off. In the bedroom, they pulled loose-fitting clothes from the closet and dressed, put on sandals, and headed downstairs. Cory stopped Kieran and slipped the silver wolf pendant Uncle Brom helped him make around Kieran's neck. They kissed and walked hand in hand up to the main house for the ritual and dinner.

CHAPTER TWENTY

Gramps sat in the library of the main house looking over various formats of the ritual for passing the power of the Silver Witch from one generation to the next. His own father put him through a ritual of such complexity; he still didn't believe either of them came out of the ceremony with their sanity intact. Aodhfin's original investiture plans got tossed when Brom ruined his personal magic. He redesigned the ritual with Kellen in mind, ending up with a convoluted mess, which somehow fit Kellen's makeup and casting style. He read the requirements in the family grimoire again. He was a warrior, and his magic reflected the ways of the House of Beauty more than they did the style of the Oisín Clan. *Fine*, Aodhfin decided, *we will make a warrior's ritual; I will initiate Kieran using the old blood brother oath.* Aodhfin sat back in his chair with a grin on his weathered face.

Forty-eight hours of fasting for both himself and his boyfriend for a five-minute ritual. Yes, Kieran's scream of outrage and disbelief might well reach Little Rock.

The boys arrived about half an hour after Aodhfin had made his decision, and he made out the sounds of their stomachs growling as they caught the scent of dinner. Kellen showed them into the library where Brom and Aodhfin were waiting. Kieran hugged both his uncle and his grandfather before taking place in the center of the library.

"Give me your right hand, Kieran," Aodhfin said.

Kieran held out his right hand and shuddered in shock as his grandfather slashed his palm with a silver dagger before cutting his own. Gramps grasped Kieran's bleeding palm with his own bleeding palm.

"Brothers of blood and magic are we now. By this exchange of blood and magic, I, Aodhfin Oisín the Silver Witch, name you, Kieran Samuel Belle Oisín-Cooper, heir to my power and to the lineage of the Silver Witch."

"By the bonds of blood and magic, I, Kieran Samuel Belle Oisín-Cooper, accept the power, the lineage, and the responsibilities of the Silver Witch."

Silver magic swirled around the men's joined hands and was gone. Aodhfin released his grip, and Kellen wrapped Kieran's hand with a cloth to slow the bleeding while Brom did the same thing for his father. Cory still stood by the door to the library with a stunned expression on his face. He was actually the first to react to the brief ritual.

"You're done? The entire thing was over in five minutes max. I had to starve for two days for a ritual that was over in five minutes."

"Well, I couldn't keep dinner waiting. Kieran's grandmother would never forgive me," Aodhfin replied.

"Yeah, right, and she's going to be happy you slashed our hands open, got blood on the carpet, and made her favorite grandchild and his husband starve for two days. I'd say you're going to be sleeping in one of the spare bedrooms, Gramps," Kieran retorted.

The men left the library and headed for the dining room where Grams was busy setting out the last few side dishes. She stopped and stared as the Oisín men and Cory entered the dining room. Her eyes were immediately drawn to her husband's and grandson's bandaged hands. She crossed the room and took each man's hand between hers and let her Sapphire magic swirl around the wounded hand, bringing its icy, healing touch. With the magic, Kieran unwrapped his hand and flexed his fingers and palm before hugging Grams.

"Thanks, Grams. I figured you wouldn't let me suffer for long."

"I hope you boys didn't get blood on the carpet in the library."

"I didn't. Gramps was the one wielding the dagger," Kieran said, dodging a swat from Gramps.

"Ungrateful whelp," he said with a laugh as Kieran stuck out his tongue from the safe location behind his grandmother.

Cory laughed at Kieran's antics. His husband was playing around like he was twelve, not twenty-two. The whole family burst into laughter before settling down to dinner and serious planning for Kieran and Kellen's trip to the Belle estate. Neither man was looking forward to dealing with Grandmother Belle, but Kieran's attempt at the test needed to be scheduled in order for him to take control of the House of Beauty. Cory tried once again to get himself included in the trip, and Kieran once again explained the reasons Cory's coming along would be a bad idea. Eventually, everything was settled, and the family did their best to enjoy the rest of the evening before returning to their respective cabins.

Back at their cabin, Cory tried one more time to convince Kieran to take him along on the trip to the Belle estate.

"Babe, I understand we all agreed, but I can't shake the sensation something is going to happen to you, and I should be with you."

"Wolf, taking you with me would put you in danger. Grandmother and a couple of the Matriarchs still have their Silver magic, and the one-shot spell granted to women of the House of Beauty is in league with the barrier spell I cast yesterday. I might block one of them from hurting or killing you, but I couldn't stop them all."

"I want to make sure you're safe, babe."

"I realize you do, Wolf. Trust me, I'll be safer with the knowledge you're here safely behind all these barrier spells and under the direct protection of Gramps, Grams, and Uncle Brom, not to mention Billy the guard shifter." Kieran acknowledged the wolf, and Billy bumped his head into Kieran's side for attention.

"Okay, I'll be good and keep an eye on the home front."

"Thanks, Wolf. You have no idea how much your being here sets my mind at ease. Now if I can convince Grandmother as easily, all will be well."

"Well, we have a couple of days before you have to head out. You can practice your speech on me."

"I think no matter how much I practice a speech, everything will go out the window when I have to deal with the Council and Grandmother. So, I'll save you the agony of me pacing pathetically up and down the living room."

"Let's go soak in the hot tub and have some naughty fun, Mr. Cooper."

"I like your thinking, Mr. Cooper." Kieran grinned and raced off toward the back porch and the hot tub, shedding his clothes as he went.

Cory was hot on his heels with Billy at his side. The lovers were both naked as they climbed into the hot tub. Billy put his paws up on the edge, panting for attention until a wave of water washed over the edge and splashed him. The wolf rumbled deep in his throat before stalking off in a wolfish huff. The lovers laughed at the wolf and lost themselves in each other.

****

The few days after the ritual naming Kieran heir to the power of the Silver Witch passed quickly, and he found himself packing madly a few hours before he was due to depart with his father. As he was attempting to jam his tracker leathers into the duffle bag he was using to take his clothes, Cory reached around and took the heavy leathers from his husband's hands. He took them and hung them in a garment bag Grams had loaned him so Kieran's clothes wouldn't be all wrinkled when he arrived at the Belle estate. Cory quietly repacked Kieran's clothes in the garment bag before closing and folding the bag neatly in half. He placed Kieran's hand on the handle of the bag, drew him in, and kissed him one more time before sending him downstairs to meet with Kellen. Father and son hugged briefly before Kellen wrapped Cory in a hug before he and Kieran walked out to Kellen's SUV. Kieran turned and waved to Cory before getting into the passenger seat of the SUV. Father and son drove off as if they were headed to face down a dragon in its lair.

****

The trip started with strained silence between Kellen and Kieran, as both men tried to find a way back from the hurt and betrayal that had come between them. Finally, Kieran broke the silence.

"We really need to settle a few things before we get to Grandmother's estate, Dad. This whole visit has been very close to being a nightmare of epic proportions—between you and Gramps making attempts on Cory's life, the crazy tests and rituals, not to mention your stunt with the condoms during our honeymoon."

"I know I can't apologize sufficiently for my actions, especially the ones I took on my own initiative. I'm afraid I got caught up in your grandfather's enthusiasm for the prophecy when I saw how far along the path you'd already traveled. I'm not trying to excuse or justify my behavior, just explain where my thinking has been coming from."

"I don't get this fascination with the damn prophecy. There are parts of it, which can't possibly happen. I don't know what the person who first envisioned the thing was on, but silver shifters will never exist. Grams doesn't think Cory will ever shift now that his Ebony magic is gone. Still, I want you to promise me no more plotting behind my back or threatening Cory. If I wanted to live my life dealing with family intrigue and plots, I would have stayed on the Belle estate."

"I promise, Son, no more plots or intrigue against you and your family. I'm glad you kept the Oisín part of your name. Despite your grandfather's and my own actions, it really is a noble heritage."

"I know, and I'm proud of that heritage. You know I'm expecting you to start dating again and to find someone who can make you happy. Plus, I'm going to need lots of half brothers and sisters to carry on the family line."

"Once we've had a proper time to mourn your sisters—something we both need to do—then I'll think about dating. You and Cory could think about using a surrogate to make me a grandfather."

"I'll promise to think about it when we get past all the current mess we need to deal with. Bring me up to speed on where things were when you left the Belle estate. I need a rough idea of who's siding with whom."

Kellen began to review for Kieran the state of family politics within the House of Beauty, as he knew them to be when he'd left after the deaths of Kieran's youngest sisters. In particular, he warned Kieran to keep an eye on his cousin Justine Belle-O'Niall, an avid supporter of the Council of Matriarchs. Kieran listened but eventually fell asleep to the sounds of his father's voice. Hours later, Kellen nudged Kieran awake as the SUV slowed at the turn off before the gates to the Belle estate.

"You'll need to be the one to announce who we are and why we're here, Son."

"I guess we should switch places," Kieran said as his father pulled the SUV to a stop.

After switching places, Kieran drove the SUV up to the guard post where one of his cousins by marriage stood on guard.

"What business do you have here?" the guard challenged.

"Tracker Kieran Belle, returning to report to the Council of Matriarchs."

"I don't have you on the list of authorized visitors, Tracker Kieran."

"Since when is a returning Tracker required to be on the list? I'm here on a direct request from the Huntress-emeritus. Do you want to get on her bad side, Cousin?"

"No, Tracker Kieran. Let me get the gate open for you."

When the gates opened wide enough, Kieran drove the SUV through and headed for the mansion. After another half hour of driving, the massive log mansion loomed up before them. The massive house sat perched on the edge of the river, which ran through the property. Kieran sighed as he parked the SUV in front of the mansion's main doors. Two of his younger cousins came out the front doors to attend to his and his father's baggage. Both boys stopped when they recognized Kieran and bowed to him.

"Tracker Kieran, what an honor to have you back. Will you be staying long?"

"Rise, Cousins. I've told you before, I don't expect you to bow to me. How long we're staying is a decision for Honored Grandmother and the Council. Take our bags to our quarters in the Huntress' suite."

The boys scrambled to get Kieran's and Kellen's bags and carry them off to their quarters.

"You're assuming your grandmother assigned us to your mother's suite."

"No, I'm staking my claim to Mother's suite as part of pushing my position as Hunter-candidate. The time for being timid around Grandmother is over. I'm a full tracker and now the only candidate left with a rightful claim to take the test. Time for the Council to show me the respect I'm due as my mother's son and heir, and I hope they choke on the fact."

"Be careful how far you push them, Son. They still have teeth, and your grandmother's tongue didn't soften while you were off at college."

"They're about to discover the meek little boy they despised, grew up and became a man with teeth and a spine. Let's go make sure no one redirected the boys to some other set of rooms."

Inside, Kieran and Kellen came face to face with one of his great-aunts who had stopped the boys on their way to take their burdens to the Huntress' suite.

"Where do you two think you're going with those bags? The Tracker and his father are assigned to the green guest suite."

"No, Great-Aunt Hilda, the Tracker and his father will be staying in the Huntress' suite as is their right as the family of the Huntress. As my mother's only heir, I claim my right to the suite as the Hunter-candidate. Do as I asked you, boys. Matriarch Hilda, you will inform the Council I am here and will await their summons to appear, but stress this, I will only wait one day for their summons before I invite myself to Council. You are dismissed."

"Don't put on airs with me, boy. You're a tracker and nothing more."

Kieran locked eyes with his great-aunt and let his anger blaze forth in his silver eyes.

"I am so much more than you know, but I am a full tracker of the House of Beauty, Matriarch Hilda. I will, however, have the respect I am due as a full tracker of this house. If you won't give me the respect as a person, I am due respect for the position I hold. None of your sons or grandsons possesses the skills or the calling to ever be a tracker. Once again, you are dismissed, Matriarch Hilda."

Kieran crossed his arms over his chest and stared at the old woman until she finally turned on her heel and headed off to meet with the rest of the Council. When she was gone, Kieran and Kellen grinned at each other before heading to their claimed suite. Both men understood the council would keep them waiting as long as possible before summoning Kieran to appear before them.

Kieran strode the halls of his former home with a confidence beyond Kellen's experience with the young man. Beside him no longer walked the frightened boy or the teen granting everyone respect whether they deserved respect or not. This young man held himself with the confidence of a trained warrior-mage. This man will be the Silver Hunter. Kellen smiled with pride as they reached the suite of the Huntress of the House of Beauty.

The two boys opened the doors to the suite and ushered Kieran and Kellen inside. Each disappeared to a different bedroom to set down the bag they carried. When the boys returned, they started to bow to Kieran until they caught his expression and stopped mid-bow. Kieran smiled at both of them and motioned them to join him as he walked out on the balcony overlooking the river. He'd always loved this view and had spent hours often with Rosie standing out on this balcony.

"I want you to fetch your group of trainees. My father and I will have need of your services while we're here. Bring food and drinks with you when you come back, enough for everyone. If the cook gives you a hard time, tell her I'll share a secret and special recipe with her—one she's seen me make but will never figure out for herself."

"We'll be back as quick as we can, Tracker Kieran. Will you be resuming our lessons?"

"Not this visit. Things are going to be changing soon. I also need one of you to go to the archives and bring me the chronicle of the—

no, never mind. I'll go fetch the tome myself. Jonas would have hidden the book I want."

The boys scampered off to go and fetch their group mates and raid the kitchen. Kellen chuckled at the unbridled hero worship the boys had for Kieran. Even the boys who realized they had no talent worshiped the ground Kieran walked on as a full tracker. Kellen grinned as he realized Kieran didn't recognize how the boys copied his mannerisms. The boys took him as their role model, the first strong male in their life full of powerful women and cowering men.

****

Kieran was pacing the suite, waiting for the Council to summon him. The swish of his heavy leather coattails was beginning to get on Kellen's nerves. He glanced at his son and wondered if Cory shared Kieran's anxiety back at the Oisín compound through the bond they shared. As if sensing his father's question, Kieran came to a complete stop and stared into the huge mirror in the sitting room. The glass shimmered as Silver magic flowed over the surface and settled to reveal a view of Cory standing before a mirror in the boys' bedroom in their cabin. The lovers stared at each other for a moment with so much love in their eyes the emotion made Kellen tear up as he remembered what the experience was like. A lot of time had past since he'd stared at someone with equal love. The boys blew each other a kiss before the spell faded, returning the mirror to its normal function. Right on time, a knock on the door to the suite sounded before Jeremy, the oldest of the group of trainees, entered the suite.

"Tracker Kieran, the Council of Matriarchs sends their compliments but refuse to receive you. They ask you and your father move to the green guest suite."

"Thank you, Jeremy. We won't be moving. The Council's time is up anyways. Time for me to go present myself to the Matriarchs, whether they wish to receive me or not."

"Be careful, Son. I'll keep the boys here so they aren't in the line of fire."

"Thanks, Dad. I'll be back when I'm done with the Council."

Kieran strode from the room, every inch a tracker of the House of Beauty. *No*, Kellen corrected his thoughts, *every inch a hunter of the House of Beauty.*

CHAPTER TWENTY-ONE

Kieran strode into the council chamber with such force the doors slammed into the walls. The Matriarchs rose at the interruption of their meeting. All except Kieran's grandmother who remained seated in her throne-like chair. When he reached the end of the conference table, Kieran smacked his hand down on top of it, and the room echoed with the sound.

"We did not summon you, boy. A tracker does not bring business before this council."

"Shut up, Aunt Fiona. I'm not here as a tracker of the House of Beauty. I'm here as the hunter-candidate. Time is up, Grandmother. You are all out of granddaughters to send to their deaths. The pact is broken, and the mongrels of the forest murdered my sisters."

"Sit down, now! My grandson makes a valid point. We lived to witness a cursed generation when we must allow a male to test as a hunter. We must also resign ourselves to this fate. Kieran is the last of the House of Beauty. With his death, our line ends."

"I'm not dying anytime soon, old woman. I've got too much to live for. Oh, I'm so much more than my sisters."

"A disappointment is what you are, boy."

"Only to a closed-minded old woman, who couldn't do what was needed to be done before she let an entire generation of huntresses be slaughtered. Serena and Rosie both died as full huntresses. My other sisters were never given the chance to properly test. The Alpha who rules this pack now is a direct descendant of the Beast himself. I'm the only one who stands a chance to defeat him."

"Male arrogance. Your chances of defeating a monster of such an ancient a lineage are less than even your sisters."

Kieran stepped back from the table, taking a defensive stance before the assembled Matriarchs. Silver magic wrapped him for a moment to encase him in silver armor. Scythe-like blades ran from his elbows to his wrists and spanned a similar length past his hands. Many of the Matriarchs drew back in their seats. Before them stood Kieran, a figure out of legend, the Silver Hunter.

"You waste whatever Silver magic you have, boy. You should save your magic for the curs of the forest."

"I'm aware Father told you who he is, or I should say what he was. I now hold his position and all the position entails. Silver magic is mine to use at will. I am the heir to the Silver Witch. On the first full moon of August, I will test to become the Hunter of the House of Beauty. When I return, I will be the fulfillment of prophecy. I will be the Silver Hunter."

"We do not agree to let you take the test, boy."

"Will you stop me, Grandmother? Better yet, can you stop me? None of you have the power to oppose me. When I return, I will head the family council. We will be relocating, so I suggest you all start packing. Contact the family lawyers and start selling this estate."

"This is my home, and I will not leave here, boy."

"My name is Kieran Samuel Belle Oisín-Cooper, the heir to the Belle of Belle. I will no longer tolerate your tone or your attitude, Grandmother. Your days of ruling over this family are over." Grandmother Belle opened her mouth to interject, only to be silenced by Kieran. "Be quiet, I'm talking. Aunt Celeste, until I return to take the test, I leave you in charge of the family council."

Kieran started to turn when he caught a flash from the corner of his eye and spun out of the path of a throwing knife aimed at his back. His movement took him out of the path of two more knives and face to face with one of his cousin's husband. The man stood stunned by Kieran's swift movement, another knife in his hand poised to throw. Kieran lashed out with a right uppercut to the man's jaw, rocking him back. Instead of closing on the man for a physical attack, Kieran picked the man up with Silver magic and hurled him across the room to smash into one of the massive log columns, which supported the roof of the chamber. His cousin-in-law didn't rise. Silver magic blazing around him like a fiery aura, Kieran turned to face the Council of Matriarchs.

"Get him a healer!" he ordered. "Which of you put him up to such a foolish attack?"

Silence reigned around the council table as most of the women cowered in fear at the massive display of Silver magic from a man. Finally, from behind the council, a younger woman emerged from the shadows, the cousin whose husband lay unconscious at the base of the massive column. Defiance and hatred filled her expression as she faced him from across the expanse of the oaken table.

"I bid my husband defend the honor of the council and the House of Beauty."

"You send a man to defend the honor of the House of Beauty, Cousin? You trained to take the test of the huntress, Cousin. Why not face me yourself? Why didn't you go to take the test? By looking at you, you're more than old enough to have gone before most of my sisters."

"I don't possess the magic. I am considered unworthy to take the test, Cousin."

"Respect your betters, child, and address the Hunter-candidate by his title, Justine," Kieran's grandmother chided the young woman. "I will not allow family to kill family. We've lost enough family this year."

"Thank you, Huntress-emeritus. Come forward, Cousin Justine, I will check if you are lacking the magic or if the magic is dormant in your branch of the family."

A healer entered the room and crossed to the unconscious man to examine him, while Justine screwed up her courage and came around the table to face Kieran who still stood with his Silver magic flaring around him. As she drew closer, Kieran doused his magic and smiled at her.

"I promise, Justine, I don't bite, despite whatever tales they're telling about me around here. You are close to Celeste's age and training, are you not?"

"I am closer to her in training; age wise, I'm a year older than Selene. I married early, which slowed down my training, Hunter-candidate," Justine said with a proper bow.

"Rise, Cousin. Hold still, this may tingle a bit," Kieran said as he raised one hand wrapped in Silver magic to touch her head.

Justine shivered as the magic washed over her from head to toe. When the magic faded, Kieran smiled at her before giving her a big hug. He whispered in her ear so only she comprehended his message.

"Congratulations, Cousin, you're pregnant with a daughter. Your magic is too latent to activate, but I will open the gift in your daughter if you wish me to."

"You would do this for me after I challenged your place?"

"I'm a scary legend come to life, Justine, but I'm the only hope for the House of Beauty. I still possess one problem though I'm still gay and not likely to produce children of my own. I will give your child the gift of the main line in exchange she will be raised as my designated heir. What do you say, Cousin?"

146

"Stop, Husband! I was wrong about Hunter-candidate Kieran," Justine said, putting herself between her revived husband and Kieran. She turned her back on her husband, dropped to her knees before Kieran, and took his right hand between both of hers.

"I, Justine Belle-O'Niall, do hereby swear my fealty to Kieran Samuel Belle Oisín Cooper as my liege, and pledge my family to the service of the Belle of Belle and the House of Beauty."

Collective gasps echoed from around the council chamber as Justine gave her fealty to Kieran as if he were already the Hunter of the House of Beauty. Her husband recovered from his shock at his wife's sudden change of heart and moved to kneel beside her and do the same.

"I, James O'Niall-Belle, do hereby swear my fealty to Kieran Samuel Belle Oisín Cooper as my liege, and pledge my family to the service of the Belle of Belle and the House of Beauty."

"I, Kieran Samuel Belle Oisín Cooper, the Belle of Belle, Hunter-candidate of the House of Beauty, do here by pledge my protection to the Belle-O'Niall of Belle. I acknowledge and accept your oaths."

For a moment, Silver magic shimmered over both Justine and James before forming into a bracelet on each of their right wrists and solidified into metallic silver.

"By this bracelet, let all recognize this couple is sworn to my service and under my protection. From this day forth, they and their line will be the Belle-O'Niall of Belle. Cousins, consult with each other how you would like your boon granted."

Justine took her husband aside and gave him the news of her pregnancy along with Kieran's offer to not only grant their daughter the gift of the House of Beauty, but to also name their child his heir. James thought for a moment and added a caveat to the deal; if Kieran ever had a child of his own, their daughter was to be trained as a tracker to serve her cousin. Justine agreed, and they approached Kieran with their request.

"Hunter-candidate Kieran, we ask for the gift for our child, a daughter, and we offer her to serve as your heir should you never produce a child of your own, or to serve as tracker should an heir of the main line be produced."

"I accept your request and grant your boon," Kieran said as a small twist of Silver magic entered Justine's womb and the child within, activating the gene that gave the women of the House of

Beauty their gift of one-shot magic. "My business here is done, Huntress-emeritus, Matriarchs. I leave you to prepare for my test on the first full moon of August. Until the appointed time, I will be reachable by phone."

Kieran turned and walked out of the Council chamber. He returned to his suite where he found his father conducting a lesson on the history of the last male hunter. Kieran stopped and listened as his father recounted how the hunter defeated a terrible dark shifter who came to the Belle estate and directly challenged him. Kieran learned this version of the tale out of the hidden chronicles from Gramps when he turned fifteen and again from Great-Uncle Jonas when he turned sixteen. When Kellen finished the tale, he glanced up and caught Kieran's eye. He dismissed the boys to their regular duties and studies. One of the boys started to ask Kellen a question until he caught sight of Kieran coming to speak with his father. The boy started to bow and withdraw until Kieran stopped him with a hand on his shoulder.

"Ask your question, Cousin. Father is wise in the history of our family, for all he is an outsider," Kieran said with a wicked grin.

"I wondered why he didn't take up the mantle of the Silver Hunter. By his actions, he seems to deny his destiny."

"An excellent question, young Ian. The only answer I can give you is he was afraid. Being the Silver Hunter calls for a special person, one who can be afraid but use his fear to make himself stronger," Kellen replied.

Ian appeared as if he was going to ask another question when Kieran broke his concentration.

"In my room, you will find the ancient chronicle on the last Hunter from the special archive. Why don't you go and read while I talk to my father?" Kieran said, easing the boy in the direction of his bedroom.

"Thank you, Tracker Kieran." Ian dashed off to Kieran's room.

"Do you think letting the boy read from this version of the chronicles is a wise choice, Son?" Kellen asked.

"I don't think the knowledge should be hidden, Dad. The boys of this family need to understand they're as good as the girls. They need a role model to emulate."

"They practically worship the ground you walk on, Kieran. You're a living example of how badly the Matriarchs have treated men in this family and how a man can still achieve his dreams."

"Well, if I'm going to achieve any dreams, we need to get back to Gramps' compound so I can study the grimoire and find out if I can get Johan to tell me more about the original Beast. Not even the hidden chronicles of the House of Beauty ever mention how Beauty used her one shot of Silver magic against the Beast."

"I'm hoping he might have a clue. It's bad enough I'm going to have to put down the entire pack in the forest, including all the pregnant females. We can't have another generation of the Beast's lineage born."

"You're right, Son. I'll go pack my things, and we can leave when you're packed and ready."

"I'll be packed and ready in about ten minutes, Dad."

Both men went to their rooms and were surprised to find their luggage already packed and waiting for them. The young boy in Kieran's room glanced up from the dusty tome of the chronicles.

"We suspected you would be leaving again once you met with the Council, Tracker Kieran, so Joey and I took the task upon ourselves to get your father's and your bags packed and ready for your departure."

"Thank you. When you're finished reading, leave the book on the table. I placed a spell on the book so you can't take the thing from this room."

"Thank you, Sir."

Kieran grabbed his bag, met his father in the outer siting room, and together, they headed downstairs and to the estate's garage. After tossing their bags in the SUV, Kellen got behind the wheel and started the car. Kieran hopped in the passenger side and buckled up. They drove off without a backward glance at the massive mansion.

CHAPTER TWENTY-TWO

On the drive back to the Oisín compound from the Belle estate, Kieran's phone rang. He glanced at the number before answering and clicked accept when he recognized the call came from Richard St. Martin.

"Hello, Mr. St. Martin, how can I help you?"

"Hello, Kieran. One of my associates called to inform me he found a young woman in Bangor asking for directions to the Belle estate. She said she needed to get to the estate as if was a matter of life and death."

"Did your associate get a name from this woman?"

"She said her name is Marissa Holden."

"She's an acquaintance from school. Last, I checked she was still in Little Rock. Why did she come all the way to Maine? She has my number. Why didn't she call me?"

"My associate says she seemed compelled to find you, almost as if she is under a spell. He also said she's a shifter, and he didn't trust her reasons for asking directions to the estate of a hunting family."

"My father and I are almost to Bangor. We can meet with your associate and Marissa to find out what's going on."

"I'll text you the address where you can meet my associate. His name is Jordan Sinclair."

"Thank you, Mr. St. Martin."

"Be careful, Kieran. Something about all this seems off, even from several states away."

"We'll take every precaution, sir. Thank you for your assistance. I owe you a favor."

"I'll save the favor for a rainy day, Kieran. Call me if you need anything."

"I will, Mr. St. Martin," Kieran said as he disconnected.

His phone chimed a moment later with a text message containing the promised address.

"So where do we need to go to find this friend of yours, Son?"

"I'm programming the address into the GPS. Considering the neighborhood, we're not in a good section of Bangor, Dad."

"Seems St. Martin took the advice your mother gave him years ago to heart, and developed an information network."

"Somehow, his network seems an extensive one, almost as if he's taken over someone else's network."

"I think if he's willing to share his information with you, Son, you don't worry how he created or acquired his network."

"Your destination is on the right," interrupted the voice of the GPS unit.

Kellen pulled the SUV over into the parking lot of an old warehouse. Kieran stopped him before he got out of the car.

"I think things would be better if you stayed out here and kept an eye on things."

"I don't like the idea of you going into a meeting alone. We don't possess any information on this associate of St. Martin's," Kellen said.

"You do realize in two months time I'm going into the heart of the Belle woods alone to face down an entire pack of shifters. I think I can handle a lone human. Besides, if he works for Mr. St. Martin, he'll be one of the good guys."

"When did you get so grown-up? Be careful. If I don't bring you back home in one piece, your husband will get your nephew to bite me."

"I'll be all right, I promise."

Kieran strode away from the SUV and approached the front of the warehouse. Pulling open the door to the warehouse office let the man waiting inside get a chance to recognize him.

"I'll assume you're the tracker Richard said would be coming."

"Tracker Kieran of the House of Beauty. Mr. St. Martin tells me you're in possession of a shifter here who asked for directions to my home."

"Yeah, she's in the back office. The chick's got a mouth on her that would make a sailor blush."

"Most likely because you called her a chick or some other term she finds offensive."

"She's a shifter and a pretty dark one from her aura."

"She's a friend, and while she carries a large trace of Ebony in her, the Ebony is balanced by Emerald."

"I didn't sense any Emerald in her."

"Well, why don't you let me sort her out and get her out of your hair?"

"Sounds like a plan to me. Oh yeah, here's the key to the cuffs. She's all yours. Don't bother to lock up; the place hasn't been used in years, and the locks are all busted anyways," the man said before heading out the door.

Kieran made his way into the back office where he found Marissa sitting cuffed to a chair with a gag in her mouth. Kieran untied the gag before unlocking the cuffs. Marissa rubbed her wrists where the cuffs chafed against her skin. She rose and hugged Kieran. The close contact was enough for Kieran to sense all the dark spells wrapped around Marissa. He broke the hug and stepped back, Silver magic barely held in check.

"What the hell happened to you, Marissa?"

"The campus pack was betrayed to an Ebony mage by someone we thought trustworthy. The mage is holding Bruce and the rest of the pack hostage until I find you and bring you back to him wrapped in chains."

"And you figured the best way to do this was to head for an estate filled with people who kill shifters on sight, and ask for me by name?"

"I've been compelled. I'm still being compelled, Kieran. Believe me, if he left me enough freewill, I'd have called and begged you to come back to Little Rock to help us."

"Hold still. Let me check if I can break the spells binding you. This will hurt since your nature tends toward Ebony."

"Hurry and do this. I suffer enough each month when the change comes."

Kieran joined his hands together as if about to pray. When he pulled them apart, Silver magic flowed between them like a pulsing electric current. He lifted his hands above Marissa's head and spread his hands as he passed them along her body from head to toe. As he passed her heart, she screamed in agony while the spells anchored to her heart burned away. When Kieran finished, she sagged back into the chair for a moment to recover.

"What a relief, getting those spells broken. Thank you, Kieran."

"So what do you recall about this Ebony mage?"

"You want to do this here and now, Kieran? Surely, we can find someplace more civilized."

"Fine, we'll go to a diner in town, and you will tell me everything you recall about this mage."

"Thank you, Kieran."

Kieran led the way back to the SUV and introduced Marissa to this father, although some little nagging sensation made him introduce Kellen as his uncle instead of as his father. Was he imagining things or did a tiny flicker of Ebony go dull in her eyes? Kellen for his part played along, urging his nephew and his friend to hop in, and they were on their way out of the bad section of town. They drove for a while before Kellen pulled the SUV into an all-night diner. The three of them got out of the car and headed for the diner. Once inside, they grabbed a booth at the back of the place, ordered sodas and burgers, and waited before beginning their conversation.

"So, Marissa, what can you tell me about this Ebony mage?" Kieran asked.

"He's incredibly powerful, and several lesser mages of various colors work for him. Everyone only refers to him as the Master, and he never shows his face. He always keeps his face cloaked in shadow."

"Why does he want me?"

"One of his associates promised you would be delivered to him as a sex slave by one of the mages working for him. In part, he wants you for your beauty, but I gather from rumors that he also wants you for some ritual to break the ancient spell binding all shifters, Kieran."

"So what are his plans involving you?"

"He wanted me to plead with you to come back to Little Rock and rescue the pack. He said I needed to get you to kill the Alpha of the pack in the woods on your family estate, and then bring you and the head back to Little Rock. Once he gets both you and the head, he holds all the components to break the spell."

"Sounds more like he's trying to eliminate a troublesome ally or a dangerous opponent," Kellen added to the conversation.

"Might be, Uncle Kellen. He may have discovered he's not a strong enough Ebony mage to face me directly. I'll do what I can to help the pack out when I get back to Little Rock, Marissa. You should head back, but keep a low profile."

"I can't go back without you, Kieran. He'll kill them all if he finds I'm back and you're still here in Maine. I realize you must be planning to deal with the dark Alpha. Let me help. I can scout things out in advance for you on the next new moon. Nobody will take heed of an owl flying around the woods."

"I'm not challenging the Alpha yet, Marissa. I have to go consult some other mages about how the spell that binds shifters was cast, and even for a Silver mage, consulting the dead is a full moon spell."

"At least let me come with you. I can help with research or keep an eye out for shifters trying to sneak up on you."

"Well, I suppose we could let her stay in one of the guest cottages, Kieran," Kellen put in.

"Can you control your shift, Marissa?"

"Yes, I learned how to when I was a little girl."

"Good. I'm not keen on taking you where I'm going, but I don't have an alternative. Uncle Kellen is right. We can lodge you in a guest cabin until we're ready to make our move against the dark Alpha. Let's get back on the road. I miss Cory, and I'd like time with my husband before diving into all the research I'm going to have to do."

Kellen picked up the check and headed to the register, while Kieran and Marissa headed for the SUV. Kellen called the compound and alerted them to the unexpected guest and Kieran's rouse with identities before heading out to the car to drive back to the compound. The ride back to the compound was quiet, with only the music on the radio playing softly to break the silence. Marissa dozed in the back seat until the SUV passed through the gates of the Oisín compound and thus the barrier spells. She woke screaming as the Silver magic washed over her, challenging her presence. The SUV stopped, held by the spells, until Kieran reached back and grabbed Marissa's hand, granting her temporary passage through the barrier spells.

"Oh, God, my head fucking hurts. I've never experienced a spell of such intensity before."

"I doubt you will again, Marissa. Those spells have been woven by generations of mages. They're the reason I asked if you can control your shifting. You're not allowed to shift here. If you do, you'll break the outermost barrier, and I'll be forced to treat you like any other dark shifter and kill you."

"I promise not to shift, Kieran."

Kieran released his hold on Marissa, and she sank back in the seat. Wariness lit her eyes for a moment before she composed herself again. Neither Kieran nor Marissa were aware of what happened from miles away. The Master participated in everything via a spell buried deep in Marissa's shifter DNA. His control links were also buried in her genes. The barrier spell had burned him more so than Marissa, and he'd lost his concentration for a moment from the pain. When he refocused, his puppet was well inside the barrier, and a large log home was coming into view before her eyes. Marissa blinked and refocused on what Kieran was saying about dropping his uncle off at the main house before he took her to the guest cabin he shared with Cory.

They'd put her up with them until they cleaned and aired out another guest cabin. When the SUV stopped before the stairs to the main house, an older version of Kieran came bounding down the steps to meet them. Kieran glanced at the expression on his uncle's face and realized Brom was having too much fun over the idea of teasing his brother over the sudden change of relationship between them and Kieran. When Kieran got out of the SUV, Brom grabbed him in a fierce hug and actually lifted Kieran off his feet.

"Glad to have you home, Son. I hope the trip wasn't too much time with your uncle," Brom said as he set Kieran down.

"I survived. At least Grandmother didn't have all your faults to harp on along with my own. Dad, I'd like you to meet Marissa Holden, a friend from college."

Brom extended his hand to shake Marissa's. "A pleasure to meet a friend of Kieran's. Welcome, Marissa."

"Thank you, Mr. Belle. What a pleasure to meet you as well."

"Marissa, we don't stand on formality around here. You can call me Brom. Kieran, why don't you take Marissa to your cabin and get her settled in while your uncle and I catch up on some of what's going on?"

"Sure, Dad. Come on, Marissa. I'm sure Cory will be happy you're here."

The two young people climbed back into the SUV and headed off to the cabin where Kieran was living with Cory. The crunch of the SUV's tires on the road alerted Billy, who started howling from the front porch of the cabin until Cory appeared beside him in a pair of shorts. Marissa regarded Kieran, watching his face light up as he caught sight of Cory, and her heart grew heavy thinking of Bruce and the other members of her pack chained up in the Master's cells.

Kieran hopped out of the vehicle and rushed up the stairs to engulf Cory in a hug and a deep kiss. Kieran broke the embrace and gestured over his shoulder, so Cory spotted Marissa climbing from the SUV. Billy's hackles raised, and his pants of joy changed to growls of warning as he bared his fangs. Kieran reached down and put his hand on Billy's head.

"Everything's okay, Billy. She's not going to hurt anyone."

The boy/wolf didn't appear convinced as he settled down on his back haunches. Marissa grabbed her bag and approached with care. Even Cory appeared leery of her presence. She passed Billy and gave Cory a brief hug before going inside to wait in the living room of the cabin.

"Why is Marissa here, babe?" Cory asked.

"Safest place to keep someone you don't trust is where you can keep an eye on them, Wolf. She's been under the control of the dark mage we've been hearing about, and I'm not sure I broke all the spells on her."

"Wouldn't we be better of tossing her on a bus back to Little Rock?"

"I'm not sure. This mage is holding the rest of the campus pack hostage against Marissa's success. Until we possess more information, I'm afraid we're stuck with her."

"I'll leave the decision up to you, Kieran. Let's get her settled into the downstairs guest room, and we can all get ready for dinner at the main house."

"Yes, I've got a lot to discuss with Dad and Uncle Kellen, not to mention Gramps," Kieran said, cluing Cory in on his deception.

"Of course, your dad's been showing me some tricks with the forge, but Grams is a miracle worker in the kitchen, and she's kept me occupied helping her in the gardens and cleaning vegetables."

"She's taken a real shine to you. Come on, I want to grab a quick shower before dinner," Kieran said before giving Cory a quick kiss and heading inside.

While Kieran went upstairs, Cory showed Marissa to the downstairs guest room, got her fresh towels, and made sure she settled in.

"Dinner is in about half an hour up at the main house with Kieran's family."

"Okay, I'll freshen up and be ready to go in a few minutes. I'm sorry to intrude on you guys like this. I guess having an unwanted guest show up wasn't how you planned to welcome your husband home."

"Not in the slightest. You understand Kieran will do whatever is needed to rescue the rest of the campus pack. He has a soft spot in his heart for your little zoo."

"Says the big bad wolf! Who would ever imagine a shifter shacking up with a tracker from the House of Beauty? You're as much of a lapdog as your nephew out in the hall."

"Unlike Kieran, Marissa, I've never cared for you or your pack of misfit shifters. You have no idea how many generations my family has spent trying to purge the taint of being a shifter from our bloodline. You, Bruce, and the rest of the merry menagerie enjoy reveling in your shifter heritage. Get ready for dinner; we'll leave in ten minutes."

Cory turned and stalked out of the room. He headed upstairs to join Kieran in a fast shower and to get ready for dinner. Kieran sensed the deep mood Cory was in and opened his arms to his husband. They hugged under the water for a few moments before Kieran turned the shower off and dried them both off. They dressed in silence and headed downstairs where they met up with Marissa and a still growling Billy. The group left the cabin and piled into the SUV for the drive back up to the main house. Silence hung thick in the passenger compartment of the SUV on the short drive to the main house. Kieran parked and everyone got out to climb the stairs up to the front doors where Brom and Kellen waited for them. They escorted the group in to the dining room and showed them to their seats at the expanded table. Kieran introduced Marissa to his grandparents before the family and guest sat down to dinner.

Tension mounted around the table as the members of the Oisín clan tried to keep from lashing out at the dark shifter sitting at their table. Marissa's presence was an affront to everyone but Kieran, even though he was worried about what her true motives were and how free from the dark mage's influence she was in reality. He rose to help Grams clear the table and bring out dessert. As he walked back into the dining room, hands full of the chocolate cake Grams baked to welcome him home, he sensed the tension snap as Marissa grabbed up a stray steak knife and slashed across his grandfather's throat. Blood spurted everywhere as Grams screamed behind Kieran, and time slowed to a crawl as Marissa threw the knife at Brom before diving for the open window, shifting as she went through. Kieran came out of his shock as he experienced the outer barrier shatter under the ancient condition, which allowed the barrier to exist. He regarded his father and uncle trying to stop the bleeding from his grandfather's wound before diving out the window in pursuit of Marissa. As he rolled to his feet from his dive, he spotted a huge gray owl stooping to try to rake him with her claws. Silver fire leapt from his hand, forcing Marissa to veer off from her attack. While he never amounted to much of an archer, Kieran's training included all weapons. Magic answered his will and formed into a silver bow and a silver arrow. As Marissa wheeled for a second pass, Kieran drew back the magic bowstring and fired. The Silver magic arrow sliced through Marissa's right wing, and she whirled, trying to stay airborne. Ebony fire wrapped around her as Kieran drew back a second arrow. Marissa vanished from sight, and the Ebony magic faded away. Kieran cursed, trying to get a sense of where Marissa went. He reeled as a huge surge of power flooded into him. His scream ripped the air as the mantle of the Silver Witch settled around him. The power burned as it flowed into the channels created in him during the rituals.

Part of Kieran urged him to race back into the house and to the dining room, where somehow he knew he'd find his family kneeling beside the body of his grandfather. The magic of the Silver Witch showed him the scene inside: blood soaked the ancient carpet beneath the old man, who'd taught Kieran so much wisdom. Grams knelt beside her fallen husband; despite her efforts, Sapphire magic had failed to heal her beloved husband. Kieran saw the deep wound in his grandfather's throat and realized only a powerful Emerald mage would stand a chance of healing such as the one that claimed Gramps' life.

Kieran locked down his emotions for his grandfather, shoving them into the same place as his unshed tears for his sisters, before he redirected his new powers. The magic showed him his family drawing together to support Grams. Mere moments had passed as he refocused and cast his senses far and wide, trying to find Marissa. He sensed her darkness along with a deeper darkness in the one place he couldn't afford a dark shifter armed with dark objects. She appeared in the central clearing where Rosie's sword held the power of the inner barrier in place. Even as he moved to stop her, he projected a fragment of his new powers into his family.

"I'm sorry, this is all my fault. I'm going to set this as right as I can, but I need you all safe, and here isn't a safe place."

"Kieran, this is not your fault. How would anyone predict she would attack your grandfather?" Kellen said, reaching for his son.

"Her actions don't matter. They sent her to capture or kill me. I'm sending you to the cave now. She's about to shatter the second barrier, and my guess is a horde of shifters are waiting to overrun this place. When you arrive, weave the strongest wards you can manage over the entrance."

"Kieran, don't send us a—" Cory didn't get to finish his sentence as Silver magic wrapped around Kieran's family, and they vanished from the house.

The surviving Oisín found themselves on the ledge at the entrance to the seaside caves where Cory and Kieran spent a week not long ago. Brom ushered the family inside and raised the first barrier by triggering the wards already built into the place. He swapped with Kellen the task of escorting their mother out of harm's way. Kellen raised powerful wards along the passageway. Nothing left for them to do but wait.

INTERLUDE: THE MASTER INTERVENES

In his lair, far away from the Oisín compound, the Master gloated over the death of the old man as he sensed the man's life and power vanishing. His renegade hunter and the various dark shifters he recruited paced around the edges of the barrier spells. They advanced when the ancient outer barrier went down, only to lose one of their numbers as the cougar shifter slammed into the second barrier and burned to ash. The Master risked revealing his location, wrapped the wounded Marissa—still in her owl form—in an Ebony transport spell, and deposited her in the clearing holding the sword, which powered the second barrier. Beside her appeared the bag of items enchanted with Ebony magic. Under his total control, she shifted back to human form and began to wrap the sword in dark magic.

CHAPTER TWENTY-THREE

Unused to the new channels of magic, Kieran crashed into the clearing as he released the transport spell and realized he'd arrived too late to stop Marissa from destroying the barrier. He shuddered when the spell shattered as he cast silver fire at Marissa, driving her back from the rapidly melting sword. He stalked into the clearing as Marissa rose to face him.

"This time you can't escape, Marissa. Your death is going to be slow and painful."

"My death doesn't matter. You'll all be as dead as the old man soon. I served my purpose in the Master's plan."

"Burn in hell, shifter scum," Kieran screamed as the ancient knowledge of the Silver Witch showed him a powerful spell. The raw power burned through him; making Kieran scream in pain before he locked down the new channels, sealing off the powers he'd inherited with his grandfather's passing.

Silver magic wrapped around Marissa, binding her in chains, which burned her everywhere they touched bare flesh. Slowly, the chains tightened, burning deeper and deeper into her flesh and toward her bones. Kieran turned and walked away, knowing Marissa was finished. Time to face the dozens of other shifters headed his way. Kieran raced for the main house where he figured the shifters would head first. When he arrived in front of the house, Kieran summoned his magical armor but not the scythe blades. From the house, he took his father's silver long sword.

****

In the cavern by the beach, Kellen, Brom, and Cory took turns keeping an eye on the entrance while Grams rested in the sleeping chamber. The men would check on her from time to time to make sure she rested. On one of his visits to check on Grams, Cory found her sitting up and alert.

"Can I get you anything, Grams?" Cory asked.

"Bring me up-to-date on Kieran please, Cory."

"All I can tell through our bond is he's still alive, but I think he's getting tired. Otherwise, all I sense is determination."

"As long as he's still alive, there is hope for us. Keep supporting him with your love, Cory."

"I will, Grams." Cory crossed the room and hugged Grams, trying to project not only his love, but also Grams' as well, to send to Kieran via the bond.

****

Kieran spun and dodged as he ran through the forest, trying to find a good place to make a stand. He played the ambush game as much as possible and had taken out seven or eight shifters already. When the fifth shifter went down, he sensed another change come over him, and realized he'd passed the test of the Huntress. Now, all he needed to do was survive. Knowing he'd become the Hunter for his generation freed Kieran to use his magic. Silver fire arced out, catching two shifters dead-on and leaving their smoldering corpses lying on the ground. Onward he raced, trying to find a good place to make a stand. Magic leapt from one hand while he slashed with the long sword in the other hand. Behind him, several shifters crashed through the underbrush, close on his heels. Leaping over a fallen tree, Kieran crashed to the ground as a sudden wave of exhaustion hit him and his armor flared and vanished. Kieran rose and came to a halt when he found himself surrounded by shifters. He found himself facing five shifters with only a sword, dressed in street clothes. His father's silver long sword flashed, driving back the pair before him, but leaving him open to the trio behind him. They jumped him, claws raking fire across his back and legs. Kieran cursed not having his leathers or enough energy to re-summon his armor, and barely managed to throw off the shifter pinning him to the ground. He rolled and slashed at an exposed foreleg with the long sword. Goddess, if only he had his sabers. He bit back a scream as his wounded back rolled across an exposed root. Kieran's attempt to rise put him off-balance, and a cougar shifter pounced, sinking its teeth into his thigh.

Never had Kieran experienced such pain. Ebony fire burned through his flesh and blood, and Kieran experienced his lock on his grandfather's magic falter. Another shifter darted in, clamping its jaws on his right wrist with enough force to break the bones, and causing him to loose his grip on the sword. Sensing their prey was weakening, the next shifter lunged for Kieran's throat, while its partner sank its teeth into Kieran's right calf. Slowed by pain and the disruption of his magic, Kieran barely managed to get his left arm up and between his throat and the shifter's jaws. A dark shadow leapt in from the left and locked its jaws on the shifter trying to get to Kieran's throat. Kieran was crippled, and the shifters recognized the condition as they circled, trying to get past the dark wolf, which blocked their path. Kieran spotted the collar around the wolf's throat and recognized Billy.

"Billy, run. Go find Cory on the beach. Go now. My magic is about to explode."

Billy glanced at Kieran and bolted straight for the lead shifter, throwing the beast off its chosen path. The shifters circled in for the kill, and Kieran prayed Billy was far enough away.

His failing mind flashed to the memories pulled from Rosie's sword about her death and her bravery. Kieran thought Rosie spoke to him in his poison ravaged mind. *Go out fighting, big brother. Take the bastards with you.*

Kieran's also thought to himself, *I'm sorry, Gramps. I failed to get them all. I can't die with no one to take my place. Cory, I love you.*

Kieran's final coherent thought ripped through the Ebony poison of the shifters' bites and unlocked all the powers of the Silver Witch and unleashed the ancient Silver magic in one titanic blast of energy. The area around Kieran for a hundred yard radius was blasted into ruins. Trees shattered and burned; the shifters vanished in blood-red explosions as devastation radiated from Kieran's shattered body. Mercifully for Kieran, he passed out before the giant pine tree fell on him, breaking both legs and pinning him to the ground.

****

As Kieran brought down the forest, his agony and desperation smashed into Cory, who let out a blood-curdling scream, which transformed in the middle into an anguished howl. For the first time ever in his twenty-six years, he shifted shape into a beautiful silver wolf. Kellen and Brom tried to calm the agitated beast down, but Cory growled and snapped at them, trying to get past them to the exit. Grams stepped out of the sleeping chamber at this moment and went to her knees, opening her arms to Cory. The silver wolf gently thrust his head into her arms and whimpered as she stroked his fur.

"Reach for him, *mac tíre óg*. Find Kieran and find your humanity. I won't let anything happen to you. Come back to us for Kieran's sake." Grams rocked the wolf until he transformed into a sobbing and naked Cory.

Brom found a pair of shorts the boys must have left on their last visit. He helped Cory dress. Kellen gathered them all and urged them to the entrance of the cavern where they found a howling Billy. Cory did for Billy what Grams had done for him, and the wolf eventually took Cory's wrist in his jaw, tugging him in the direction that led back to the forest and the main house. The party of survivors followed the wolf back to the forest where they witnessed firsthand the destruction wrought by Kieran's magic. They picked their way carefully through the fallen trees and around the smoldering stumps until Billy lead them to a giant fallen pine. With a cry, Cory leapt toward the pine and landed beside Kieran's mangled body. Somehow, despite all the burning trees, Kieran's beautiful hair remained untouched. Cory called out to the others.

"He's over here under this tree. He's barely breathing."

Grams took charge, using her magic to stabilize Kieran, while Kellen and Brom worked to get the tree off him.

"Kellen, do you have enough power to transport us to the hospital?" Grams asked.

"No, Mother. Father severed my connection to the powers of the Silver Witch, so Kieran would have everything if anything happened to him. I can get you, Kieran, and myself back to the house, and we can load him in the van. Can you keep him stable long enough to get to the emergency facilities at Mount Desert Island Hospital in Bar Harbor?"

"I'll have to do my best, even if I need to lower his temperature until he's in a coma."

"Brom, you and Cory will have to go by foot back to the main house. Take the SUV and meet us in Bar Harbor."

"We'll be as close behind you as we can manage," Brom replied as Kellen began the transport spell, wrapping the magic around his mother and son as well as himself.

"Come on, Cory, we need to be around when they get to the hospital."

"Kieran will need clothes, and I'd better grab something besides these shorts."

"Your cabin is on the way. We'll pack a bag with clothes for both of you."

Cory, Brom, and Billy raced back toward the cabin. The real race, the one against death, had just begun. *Would they be able to get Kieran to medical treatment in time? Could the doctors save Kieran?* Cory wondered as he put on more speed, trying to get back to Kieran's side.

PLACE OF INTEREST MENTIONED IN WITCH

Cory mentions in the story that he found the diamond for the ring he gives Kieran at Crater of Diamonds State Park back in Arkansas. This Arkansas State Park is unique among diamond sites anywhere in the world. It is open to the public and is the only site where you can hunt for diamonds and keep what you find. The diamonds from this park come in three colors: white, brown, and yellow. As I was writing *Witch,* a park visitor found an 8.52-carat white diamond, which became the new record holder for the fifth largest diamond found at the park since the property became a state park in 1972. For more information about Crater of Diamonds State Park and other Arkansas State Parks, visit www.ArkansasStateParks.com.

ABOUT THE AUTHOR

Kethric Wilcox (1966-) was born in Melrose, Massachusetts to average middle-class parents. Growing up, he did normal kid things, cub scouts, and boy scouts, earning the rank of Eagle Scout. He graduated high school, went to college as a computer graphic design major—in the days when the field was more programing than design—for a while before dropping out to go work in the travel and tourism industry for four years. Kethric relocated to Little Rock, Arkansas in the early 1990s and went back to college, earning a B. A. in both graphic design and history. He currently lives with his partner, whom he officially started dating in 2008, in a 1923 house they renovated in 2012, and works as a graphic designer doing museum and trail exhibits. In his spare time, Kethric writes church dramas and paranormal gay romances. When he's not at a computer, writing, designing, or doing research, Kethric enjoys playing in the kitchen, creating healthy versions of some of his favorite desserts and dinners. He is an avid camper and loves to get away from technology from time to time to recharge his spiritual and creative energies.

THE STORY CONCLUDES IN:

HUNTER
LEGEND OF THE SILVER HUNTER
BOOK THREE

BEAUTY'S TALE

He was within thirty miles of his own house, thinking on the pleasure he should have in seeing his children again, when going through a large forest he lost himself. It rained and snowed terribly; besides, the wind was so high, that it threw him twice off his horse, and night coming on, he began to apprehend being either starved to death with cold and hunger, or else devoured by the wolves, whom he heard howling all round him, when, on a sudden, looking through a long walk of trees, he saw a light at some distance, and going on a little farther perceived it came from a palace illuminated from top to bottom. The merchant returned God thanks for this happy discovery, and hastened to the place, but was greatly surprised at not meeting with any one in the outer courts. His horse followed him, and seeing a large stable open, went in, and finding both hay and oats, the poor beast, who was almost famished, fell to eating very heartily; the merchant tied him up to the manger, and walking towards the house, where he saw no one, but entering into a large hall, he found a good fire, and a table plentifully set out with but one cover laid. As he was wet quite through with the rain and snow, he drew near the fire to dry himself. "I hope," said he, "the master of the house, or his servants will excuse the liberty I take; I suppose it will not be long before some of them appear."

He waited a considerable time, until it struck eleven, and still nobody came. At last, he was so hungry that he could stay no longer, but took a chicken, and ate it in two mouthfuls, trembling all the while. After this he drank a few glasses of wine, and growing more courageous he went out of the hall, and crossed through several grand apartments with magnificent furniture, until he came into a chamber, which had an exceeding good bed in it, and as he was very much fatigued, and it was past midnight, he concluded it was best to shut the door, and go to bed.

It was ten the next morning before the merchant waked, and as he was going to rise, he was astonished to see a good suit of clothes in the room of his own, which were quite spoiled; certainly, said he, this palace belongs to some kind fairy, who has seen and pitied my distress. He looked through a window, but instead of snow saw the most delightful arbors, interwoven with the beautifullest flowers that were ever beheld. He then returned to the great hall, where he had supped the night before, and found some chocolate ready made on a little table. "Thank you, good Madam Fairy," said he aloud, "for being so careful, as to provide me a breakfast; I am extremely obliged to you for all your favors."

The good man drank his chocolate, and then went to look for his horse, but passing through an arbor of roses he remembered Beauty's request to him, and gathered a branch on which were several; immediately he heard a great noise, and saw such a frightful Beast coming towards him, that he was ready to faint away.

"You are very ungrateful," said the Beast to him, in a terrible voice; "I have saved your life by receiving you into my castle, and, in return, you steal my roses, which I value beyond any thing in the universe, but you shall die for it; I give you but a quarter of an hour to prepare yourself, and say your prayers."

The merchant fell on his knees, and lifted up both his hands, "My lord," said he, "I beseech you to forgive me, indeed I had no intention to offend in gathering a rose for one of my daughters, who desired me to bring her one."

"My name is not My Lord," replied the monster, "but Beast; I don't love compliments, not I. I like people to speak as they think; and so do not imagine; I am to be moved by any of your flattering speeches. However, you say you have got daughters. I will forgive you, on condition that one of them come willingly, and suffer for you. Let me have no words, but go about your business, and swear that if your daughter refuse to die in your stead, you will return within three months."

The merchant had no mind to sacrifice his daughters to the ugly monster, but he thought, in obtaining this respite, he should have the satisfaction of seeing them once more, so he promised, upon oath, he would return, and the Beast told him he might set out when he pleased, "but," added he, "you shall not depart empty handed; go back to the room where you lay, and you will see a great empty chest; fill it with whatever you like best, and I will send it to your home," and at the same time Beast withdrew.

"Beauty and the Beast," Jeanne-Marie LePrince de Beaumont, English translation, 1757

Mother, never refuted this section of the tale. She loved her father, the last man she ever really loved, and I think she wanted to remember him as someone who loved her after the rest of her family abandoned her to her fate. Rumors abound about the youngest of my uncles, Johann, having a destiny he chose not to face or was forbidden to face by Grandfather. Whatever the case may be, Johann gifted mother with the ability to channel Silver magic once in her lifetime in her greatest hour of need. We all suspect she used her spell during the fight with the Beast, but even on her deathbed, she wouldn't revel what she'd done with the spell. Father past many years before mother. I believe his fear of her kept him from revealing the truth.

From the First Chronicle of the House of Beauty, translated from the original French, 1998

PROLOGUE: THREE WEEKS AGO

John Mason was surprisingly excited when he got off the phone with Kieran Belle. The boy's excitement about his upcoming wedding and handfasting was contagious it seemed. The photography professor dialed his travel agent to arrange for a trip to Maine. As he gave the travel agent his details, John wandered through the living room and stopped before the photographic portrait of Kieran's fiancé hanging over the fireplace. A shirtless Cory Cooper leaning on a piece of construction equipment looked back at the professor with a deeply felt love for the man on the other side of the camera. The boys hadn't even begun to admit their feelings for each other when the picture had been taken, but you didn't have to even know them to sense what they felt in that moment in time. John's daydreaming was broken by the voice of his travel agent.

"Sir, are you still there?"

"Yes, I'm sorry, my mind wandered off. What were those flight times again?"

The agent rattled off the flight information between Little Rock and Bangor, Maine along with the cost. John agreed and added in a rental car booking and then gave the agent his credit card information. The agent let him know his reservations were complete and his tickets would be delivered in a couple of days. John thanked the man and hung up. He decided he'd call Kieran back when he had his tickets in hand.

For upcoming releases and more about the World of the Silver Hunter books, follow Kethric's blog, World of the Silver Hunter, at http://www.kethricwilcox.com.

On Twitter @KethricW

OTHER TITLES BY KETHRIC:

Tracker: Legend of the Silver Hunter, Book One.

Once upon a time there was Beauty and there was the Beast. The spinners of tales would have you believe these two fell in love and lived happily ever after.

The spinners lied!

The Beast was a shifter and Beauty became a huntress and founded a long line of huntresses aided by the power of silver magic.

Kieran Belle is a descendant of the House of Beauty and a tracker who longs to live a life free of killing shifters. Aided by his father he escapes to college in Little Rock, Arkansas where he meets the boy of his dreams, Corwin Cooper.

Corwin Cooper is a descendant of a clan of shifters, who has never shifted himself. Having finally decided to go to college, Corwin arrives and meets the mate his inner wolf cries out to claim for his own in Kieran Belle.

Ancient prophecy says Kieran is destined to become the legendary Silver Hunter. Dark forces seek to derail prophecy and end the House of Beauty. Can a child of the shifter-hunting House of Beauty and a descendant of shifters find love and happiness or will dark forces and opposing heritage tear them apart?

www.ingramcontent.com/pod-product-compliance
Lightning Source LLC
Chambersburg PA
CBHW070921130626
46555CB00001B/226